DEAR

Dear Readers,

Love sneaks up on you when you least expect it. And believe me, I've kissed enough frogs to know that not every one is a prince! Just because a man is tall, dark and sexy, and fabulously rich, doesn't mean that he's all that.

Take my next-door neighbor Tre Monroe. He's a hunk, he makes good money (he even drives a Porsche), but the man is a D-O-G. Could it be that his playboy persona hides the soul of a romantic?

Keeping it real,

Jenna

P.S. Perhaps you *can* teach an old dog new tricks!

MARCIA KING-GAMBLE

was born on the island of St. Vincent—a heavenly place in the Caribbean where ocean and skies are the same mesmerizing blue. An ex-travel industry executive, Marcia's favorite haunts remain the Far East, Venice and New Zealand.

In her spare time, she enjoys kickboxing, step aerobics and Zumba, then winding down with a good book. A frustrated interior designer, Marcia's creativity finds an outlet in her home where nothing matches. She is passionate about animals, tear-jerking movies and spicy food. She serves double duty as the director of member services at a writers and artists institute in South Florida, and is the editor of *Romantically Yours*—a monthly newsletter.

To date, Marcia has written twelve novels and two novellas. She loves hearing from fans. You may contact her at Mkinggambl@aol.com or P.O. Box 25143, Fort Lauderdale, FL 33320.

MARCIA KING-GAMBLE

FLAMINGO PLACE

KIMANI
ROMANCE

To Emily Martin with heartfelt thanks.
You're the best unpaid assistant a woman could ever hope for.

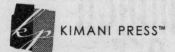 KIMANI PRESS™

ISBN-13: 978-1-58314-772-6
ISBN-10:   1-58314-772-1

FLAMINGO PLACE

Copyright © 2006 by Marcia King-Gamble

www.kimanipress.com

Printed in U.S.A.

Dear Reader,

Welcome to Flamingo Beach, where the living is easy. Nothing ever changes here except for the population.

If you're young and single, Flamingo Place, the fancy new condominium, is where it's at. You'll need to be over thirty though, and you can't have children. Plus your income needs to be in a high bracket. Of course you could lie about that.

Flamingo Beach has just about everything to keep a body happy. We have restaurants, churches and beauty shops. Our inhabitants are friendly—notice I didn't say nosy. We also have a florist. Yup, the mayor's son and his lover are partners in a florist shop.

That, by the way, is how this story came about. Jen, the new advice columnist at the *Chronicle*, used a word to describe our florist and people got ticked. D'Dawg, a hot radio personality, jumped all over her, and the two went at it. Rumor has it they've since made up....

If you'd like more information about Flamingo Beach, write to me at P.O. Box 25143, Fort Lauderdale, FL 33320, or e-mail me at mkinggambl@aol.com.

Don't be strangers now. Come down for a visit!

Marcia King-Gamble

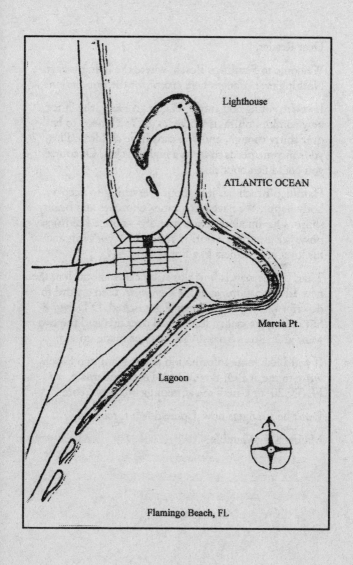

Lighthouse

ATLANTIC OCEAN

Marcia Pt.

Lagoon

Flamingo Beach, FL

Chapter 1

*Y*ou *say your son is queer! Maybe he's a confirmed*
bachelor or simply set in his ways.

Thump! Thump! Thump! The damn boom box next
door was driving Jen St. George crazy.

Determined to ignore the loud rap music emanating
from her neighbor's apartment, Jen continued to type.
Her next door neighbor was the most inconsiderate
person she'd ever encountered and by far the rudest.

Jumping up, Jen banged on the wall and yelled,
"Can you turn down your music?"

When her request didn't produce the desired

results, Jen called to her assistant, Chere, "Turn on the stereo, please. Loud."

Jen's attention returned to the letter she was working on. She banged out words no sooner than they'd popped into her head. This was her tenth letter of the day, and she was exhausted from dispensing advice. The moniker *love diva* hadn't been earned easily.

The script in front of her was beginning to blur and tiny black dots were popping out in front of her eyes. On any given day being an advice columnist wasn't easy, but she loved her job and got immense satisfaction from helping people. Giving advice had made her a popular and sought-after teenager. It had felt good to be needed. Today it still did.

"Chere, where are you? You're supposed to be turning on the stereo," Jen called, her irritation at her assistant reflecting in her tone. Not that Chere would even get it.

"I hear you," her assistant called from the vicinity of the kitchen.

Dear Jenna made a living as an advice columnist to the lovelorn. This career came with a huge responsibility. People trusted her to choose their life partners or help them dump an inconvenient relationship. She was considered the diva of love because her advice

Marcia King-Gamble 9

was seldom off the mark. Normally her readership loved her in-your-face style.

The deafening music continued from next door. Jen thumped on the wall again.

"Please show some consideration. Jerk," she muttered under her breath.

Jen turned on her own stereo, making sure her volume matched 5B's. Now she could barely hear herself think.

Back at her desk Jen considered changing the wording of her response. Conservative Flamingo Beach, the small North Florida town where she now lived, might not get *Dear Jenna*'s hip-happening style. She really meant no harm; if anyone knew her family situation they would know that.

No, better to leave it like that. Maybe she'd bring this sleepy oceanfront community into the twenty-first century. The word *queer* was perfectly acceptable and in vogue now. It was totally embraced by the gay community. The TV show *Queer Eye for the Straight Guy* had made the word a household name, and it was one of the more popular shows around.

Still, there was always the chance some uninformed reader could interpret it as a slur, especially in a backwoods Southern town. She was on ninety-day probation at *The Flamingo Beach Chronicle*. The newspaper had wooed her way from Ashton, Ohio, an even smaller Midwest town.

In a relatively short time, Jen had acquired quite the following and *The Chronicle*'s circulation had increased. The competition, *The Southern Tribune,* was watching them closely. Of course her boss hadn't said word one to her about this accomplishment. He dispensed compliments meagerly, just as she'd been warned he dispensed raises.

The loud noise next door continued. Jen glanced at her full to overflowing in-box and sighed. What on earth was taking Chere so long? She'd excused herself to use the bathroom earlier and must have detoured to the kitchen.

Chere was to have read and catalogued the mail by now but she'd arrived late as usual, leaving Jen to handle most of it herself. Two days a week they worked from home—Jen's home. This was supposed to allow them to keep up with correspondence. But something needed to be done about Chere Adams—and soon. There had to be better qualified administrative assistants around.

"Chere!" Jen shouted over the din emanating from next door. "What's the holdup?"

"I said I was coming."

Jen rolled her eyes. Sure she was, when she was

good and ready. There was a residential directory somewhere around. Jen searched and found it before realizing she didn't know the neighbor's name. This meant she'd have to go next door.

The hall was alive with music. Using her fist, she banged on 5B's front door.

"What's up?" he called when the sound registered.

She didn't stick around to answer. Hopefully he would get the message. Rather than wasting energy debating his selfishness, Jen returned to reread Ms. Mabel's letter. The old lady had a quirky sense of humor. She pleaded with Jen to help save her son, even likening homosexuality to a rare disease.

How had she come to such a conclusion? It was a metrosexual world. Men got manicures, pedicures and facials just like women did these days. Men were marrying later and later. Thirty-five wasn't that old. Jen was thirty-two and very single, and left to herself she'd stay that way. There had to be more to it. Maybe Mother Mabel had found her son in a compromising position. Jen decided she would ask.

She typed her witty and well-thought-out prose, pausing to rotate her cramping shoulder muscles and stare out the living room windows. A beautiful coral and lavender sunset made her long to be outdoors, sipping on something cool and frothy. It was wishful thinking on her part—with the looks of that in-box.

It had taken Ms. Mabel a full eight pages to tell how her son had been engaged three times but never quite made it down the aisle. Mama was now speculating that her son's loud "Cabana Boy" shirts and "butt-hugging" jeans were a clear sign he was batting for the other team.

The music next door ceased, thank God. Jen's head still vibrated with the sound. She squared her shoulders and took a deep breath. She'd never regretted leaving Ashton, the small Midwest town where she'd worked for ten years. *The Flamingo Beach Chronicle*'s offer had come at the perfect time.

Jen's romantic life had been in turmoil. She'd been happy to put space between herself and Anderson, the lying, cheating dog who'd broken her heart and put her off men, permanently. Now was not the time to think of him. She had a deadline to meet.

"I'm calling it a day," huffed Chere, the assistant she'd inherited. She was still chomping on the chicken leg she'd taken from Jen's refrigerator. She slid a glass of water Jen's way. "Unless you need me for something." Two plump cheeks parted to reveal perfectly white teeth. Then she made a chicken neck. "What's with that brother? He tone deaf or what?"

Damn if she knew. She'd been wondering the same thing. Jen waved an expansive hand in the direction of her crowded desk. "Nope, just self-focused like we need to be. We've got work, girl. Those letters need to be read and logged in. Today."

Chere placed two pudgy hands bedecked with gold rings on each finger on her oversized hips. Her nails were a work of art, depicting the New York skyline in black and silver. She proudly announced to anyone who would listen that she'd grown up in the Bronx, followed a man South, and although that relationship was long over with, remained because she enjoyed the Southern hospitality. Translation, the dark-skinned brothers had been good to her and delighted in her charms.

"Shoot. I have plans tonight," she grumbled. "What am I supposed to tell Leon?"

"What you've told every man you didn't want to be bothered with. You're busy."

"But I want to be bothered with this one—you should see how he's hung...."

Jen now fixed her hazel-eyed stare on the outrageous woman who thought work was a contagious disease and tended to disappear more often than not. Chere did serve a purpose though. She knew everything there was to know about Flamingo Beach and its residents. She'd slept with most of the men and could proudly list their long and shortcomings. As she'd said to Jen time and time again, you didn't have to be skinny as a rail to bag a man. Booty was booty. Good loving just as easily came in an oversized package.

Chere harrumphed before settling in and attacking the pile in the in-box. She slid a nail that reminded Jen of a talon under one envelope flap while sighing loudly.

"You might as well get used to long hours. If we'd met at a small Midwest paper you do everything including your own copyediting," Jen added.

"I'd rather be serving fries at Mickey Dee's," Chere grumbled. "Here you are, stuck in this big ass apartment when you should be lying around the pool sipping on Margaritas and strategizing how to get one of them personal trainers into bed. My mama used to say no employer's ever dedicated a tombstone to a workaholic. Hell, you're lucky to get a silver watch if you make it to retirement."

Jen smothered a grin. Lazy as Chere was she did provide comic relief. "Here, take a look at this." Jen flipped Ms. Mabel's letter in Chere's direction. "What's your take?"

Chere's double chins bobbed. She scanned the

letter before guffawing loudly. "Uhhh, your advice ain't going to sit well with the peoples."

"Why not?"

"Because this is Buppyville. We are nothing if not politically correct. These peoples aren't going to like that you used 'queer.' Lover boy might be a player but you telling Mama to get on the Internet and place one of them there ads is meddling, baby girl. No man ever likes the babe Mama chooses."

"Maybe you should be answering my mail," Jen said jokingly. "You know how this town operates and you seem to know your way around men."

"Yup, I sure as hell do. What if Romeo's gay? You didn't tackle that."

Jen chuckled. "Maybe the number of letters from women offering to turn him straight will force him out of the closet."

"I doubt that. I had me a few of them, even my antics couldn't keep them on the straight and narrow. Listen, I have to go. Leon will kill me for being late." She tossed the letters back on Jen's desk and reached for an oversized Coach bag in a sickly shade of coral, hoisting it onto her shoulder. "Just tell the witch to butt out of a grown man's life. She should be at bingo or learning to fox trot at Arthur Murray. She needs to get a life."

Chere wiggled her bejeweled fingers and headed for the door. "Want me to take care of homeboy next door on my way out?"

"I already have."

No sooner had Chere left than the cacophony next door started again. Jen's walls vibrated. Her head felt like someone had parked a Mack truck in it and left the motor running. Enough was enough. Jen stepped out into the hallway in time to see a scantily clad hoochie mama exit 5B.

This was no tenant. 5B seemed to get more than his share of action. Women were constantly coming and going at all kinds of hours. Jen had heard the fights, the broken glasses and the slammed doors.

"Call me," the woman with the belly-button ring said to someone Jen couldn't see.

A grunt followed before the door closed firmly behind her.

Jen's Midwestern good manners kicked in. "Hello," she greeted the woman tottering by in too-high heels.

A disinterested glance was tossed Jen's way. She'd been summarily dismissed as inconsequential. The music inside 5B's apartment ended abruptly.

Jen returned to her apartment and decided to get comfortable. She slid into a pair of shorts and a halter top and considered what to do about dinner. There were at least three restaurants to choose from nearby but it was no fun sitting at a table eating alone.

Discarding the possibility of having food delivered, Jen opened the refrigerator hoping to find something edible. She slammed the door again. It looked like takeout was the only option.

The Godawful racket started again. Now it sounded like Middle Eastern chanting. 5B had turned up his boom box full volume again. An Indo rap artist was going on about bitches and whores.

Grabbing the remote phone, Jen punched in the numbers for a soul food restaurant that delivered and shouted her order. She would try escaping the loud music by taking the pile of mail out to the terrace.

Jen's apartment offered a clear view of the beach. Tiny white lights were starting to twinkle on the opposite shore. On a sigh, she inhaled the smell of brine and thought how lucky she was.

The pounding music followed her outside. This new singer sounded like a cat in heat.

"You just got on my last nerve," Jen mumbled, tossing the letters aside. "I have a right to a peaceful existence and I'll have it if it's the last thing I do."

Tre Monroe snorted loudly. He was bored out of his skull. He needed constant stimulation. These wannabe artistes were not doing it for him. He'd hoped to find at least one potential star in the bunch, but nada so far.

WARP, the radio station where he was both musical director and on-air personality, was constantly inundated with unsolicited CDs; CDs that he as musical director was forced to listen to in his spare time. Tre had cranked up his music hoping that the lyrics and beat of just one of them would get his attention. But so far the pitiful talent just made him more restless than he already was.

He popped another disk into the player. He'd already had one uninvited visitor show up, a woman he'd dated casually; someone almost fifteen years his junior. At one time the sex had been good, but the conversation nonexistent. He'd quickly grown tired of her and tried to let her down gently, but she continued to hang on.

In a couple of hours he would be on the air, playing his tunes and broadcasting from the only black radio station in town: the happening station. Tre loved fielding calls from his late-night audience, often a colorful and vocal group.

Over the sounds of heavy metal, Tre vaguely registered the banging at his front door. Not her again. Had she forgotten something? Swearing softly to himself, he padded barefoot and shirtless to answer. Security was getting lax. He'd have to talk to somebody about this.

Tre ignored the peephole and threw his front door wide. The woman who stood before him looked like she had a definite axe to grind. He registered that she was attractive and had a great pair of legs. She had the kind of smooth cinnamon-colored skin you felt compelled to touch. Her lips were full, wide and inviting. Streaked, straightened hair skimmed her broad shoulders. High cheekbones and wide hazel eyes gave her a slightly exotic look. How come he'd never seen her before?

Tre's gaze slid down the woman's strong body. She was ripe. Her perfectly proportioned breasts filled that halter top nicely. Damn it but those long, shapely legs deserved to be wrapped around somebody, preferably him. He wondered how come he hadn't run into her before. He would have remembered. When he smiled at her, she did not smile back.

It dawned on him it had to be the new tenant. He'd seen the moving truck pull up and unload a pitiful few pieces of furniture; mostly antiques though, so at least she had good taste. Sheer nosiness had forced him to inquire of the moving men where they were taking them. They'd told him they belonged to the occupant of 5C.

"Is there something you wanted?" Tre asked, staring at the woman. She'd folded her arms across those luscious breasts and now they threatened to spill from the low-cut halter.

"Your music is driving me crazy. I can hardly think. Much less work."

"Who am I turning my music down for?" Tre asked, his glance sliding over her body again.

She seemed conscious of his assessment but not at all self-conscious. Yet she backed off, putting space between them. "I live in 5C," she said, pointing up the hallway. "Next door. Show a little consideration. I'm surprised 5A and D haven't called security."

Tre narrowed his eyes, giving her the look that usually made women's legs buckle. He'd been told often enough he had bedroom eyes. He swept his gaze over the tempting piece of flesh standing in front of him, letting his eyes linger for a second too long on the woman's cleavage, then focusing on those long legs again. And what legs. He'd always been a leg man.

"No one's ever complained about my music before, baby," he drawled. "I've lived here two years. You've been here how long?" One eyebrow arched upward. He was at his most intimidating.

"About six weeks," his pissed-off neighbor supplied. "Long enough to listen to noisy altercations in the hallway and develop headaches from that obnoxious stereo of yours. I work at home a couple days a week."

Tre draped an arm across the doorsill. "Who am I supposed to be shutting down my boom box for? You got a name?" On purpose he'd slipped into the dialect of the street.

5C actually had the grace to look embarrassed. She thrust a toned arm forward. She must work out with weights, another point in her favor. Toned arms with just a trace of muscle were sexy.

"Jen St. George. And you are?"

"Jen?"

Tre let the name wrap around his tongue. The last name was definitely foreign. She might be from the islands; Haiti quite possibly. He'd always had a *thang* for island girls. They were feisty and knew exactly who they were. She waited for him to tell her his name.

"Trestin," Tre said, skipping his last name as he often did. Once women found out he was WARP's music director, and popular radio personality, D'Dawg, they began acting like fools. The name was rightfully earned from his "poon hound" days.

"Well, Trestin," Jen said, "can we come to an

agreement? Can you at least lower your tunes so I can get back to work?"

The door of 5A located directly across from Tre pushed open. Ida Rosenstein stuck a head decorated with pink curlers covered by a net through the opening. She called in the loud croaky voice of a smoker, "You could at least invite this one in." Looking from one to the other, she sniffed. "How come your girlfriends never wear clothes?"

"I am not one of his girlfriends," Jen snapped. "Like you, I'm his next-door neighbor."

"What was that?" Ida shouted, lighting a cigarette and blowing a perfect smoke ring.

Jen pinched her nose. "Must you?"

Tre's palm cupped Jen's elbow. He propelled her in the direction of the smokestack. "This is Jen St. George," he said. "Jen just moved in."

"John, did you say? Why does she have a man's name?"

"My name's Jen," Jen carefully repeated. "Doesn't his music bother you? How come you're not complaining?"

"I'm too old to complain. It doesn't do any good. I just take action."

Tre tried to discreetly whisper to Jen that Ida was severely hard of hearing.

"His music," Jen shouted. "Doesn't it bother you? It's too loud."

"I like his music," Ida boomed back. Good for her. "It makes me feel alive." She began mimicking urban dance movements she must have seen on TV.

Jen was stunned.

Tre smiled brightly at Ida. She was taking up for him. He'd always liked the old lady and gave her credit for being so open-minded at her age. She'd told him she refused to move when the building was re-modeled and the first influx of black upper-middle-class tenants moved in. According to Ida, she was the first resident to move in after the building was con-structed. She'd be there until it was torn down or they took her out in a box.

A head poked out from 5D. "Can you keep it down?"

Camille Lewis was the last person Tre wanted involved in his business. Her mouth ran like there was no tomorrow. She thrived on gossip or made it up. Tre would have to convince Winston, her husband, to help put a lid on Camille's mouth. That would cost him a handful of new CDs.

"This is Jen St. George, our new neighbor," Tre said smoothly, forcing a smile. "Camille Lewis."

"We already met." Camille turned her attention back to her cell phone.

She had a heavy West Indian accent that came and went depending on whether she was talking to a relative or not. She waggled the cell phone at him. "I'm trying to talk to my girlfriend. Can you at least go inside?"

He was being ganged up on. Camille Lewis normally didn't care about how loud he played his music; just that he made sure some of the disks came her way. She'd mastered the art of multitasking and knew everything there was to know about everyone in the building. They usually got along fine and Tre had learned to ignore her monitoring of his comings and goings.

"Fine. We'll take our discussion inside," Tre agreed. He held his apartment door open hoping Jen would come in. "Night, y'all."

Camille grunted at him and slammed shut her door. Ida stayed put.

"Tomorrow this entire building's going to hear about the threesome we had in the hallway." Ida cackled loudly and stubbed her cigarette out in the ashtray she held. Examining Jen through rheumy eyes, she continued. "You're a step up from his usual. His taste is improving."

"I am not his usual. I am nothing to him," Jen answered before stomping off.

Tre said good-night to Ida Rosenstein and slipped inside his apartment.

Jen St. George wasn't going to be easy. He'd have to plan a strategy, maybe take a bottle of wine over to her later in the week and turn up the heat.

With any luck, he'd have her on her back and those long legs wrapped around him.

Give him one month and he'd be in those tight shorts of hers. Then guess who would be complaining about who.

Chapter 2

"Yo, Flamingo Beach. This is D'Dawg coming to you live from WARP. Bad day at work? You been dumped, lied to, or just played? Come sit back and chill with me. My tunes are guaranteed to make you relax and take you on a trip down memory lane to the good old days when brothas and sistahs pushed getting high on life. Let's conversate. You can tell me what's happening in this sleepy little town of ours, the Southern answer to Peyton Place."

Tre had a habit of slipping into urban vernacular when addressing his radio audience. He'd grown up in the ghettos of Detroit and knew this was what his people expected and what they understood. He punched a button and Luther Vandross's soulful crooning dominated the airwaves. The singer was a man he'd deeply admired. Tonight would be a tribute to him.

Tre sat back, preparing to listen. He propped his feet on the console and took a bite of his sandwich, letting Luther's sensual voice mesmerize him. It was times like this he wished he was with someone special, someone he had a connection with. So far that hadn't happened and he didn't want to just hook up with anyone. Times had changed and making the wrong choice came with consequences.

Another Luther song dropped, this one in a slightly different vein. As the singer began sharing his childhood memories with the radio audience, Tre unfolded *The Flamingo Beach Chronicle* and began flipping through it. This new advice columnist was a trip. Here she was giving some crazy old lady tips on marrying off her son. What if the man was a confirmed bachelor? And who cared if he was gay?

He reread the mother's letter and dissected *Dear Jenna*'s response. Pushing a button on the console he drawled, "Nothing like a little Luther to soothe the soul and get us in the groove. So what y'all think about this chick Aunt Jemima, the new advice columnist from Cincinnati? Anyone read today's column? Let's break it down. I'm here to take your calls."

Tre guffawed loudly. "Freudian slip, y'all. The lady's name is Jenna. This brotha thinks she likes to stir things up, telling the man's mama to get on the Internet and place one of them personal ads. Phone lines are open, y'all. I'll be here for the next four hours."

During the next fifteen minutes every line at WARP lit up. Tre took call after call and conceded he just couldn't keep up. His show rocked.

"Sheila, what do you think?"

"*Dear Jenna* gave sound advice."

"Why is that? What mama needs to get involved in a grown man's business?"

To her credit, Sheila stood firm. "I'm a mama. My son brings home these *hos*. They come into my house, belly hanging out, disrespecting me. Who can blame a mother for wanting to see her son settled with a good churchgoing woman?"

"I hear that. But what if the man's gay or as Jemima calls it, *queer?*" Tre now appealed to the audience. "Anybody else got anything contradictory to say?" He punched another button. "Rufus, you still hanging?"

"In for the duration, my man."

"You got a different opinion from Sheila?"

"Yeah, as a matter of fact I do. Mama needs to butt out. Cut the apron strings and let sonny boy make his own mistakes." Rufus's raucous laughter rang out. "Mama needs to find herself a man."

"Anyone else in the house?" Using a finger that was almost as dark as the console before him, Tre pressed the button on yet another line.

"This is Kim. My ex-boyfriend turned out to be gay and there was nothing I could do to change that."

"Hear that, callers. Kim couldn't get her man to change. You try one of them Victoria's Secret numbers?"

"Yes, I did…."

Kim quickly hung up. She'd lost it and sounded like she was about to cry.

And so it went on, until Tre took a break for advertising. All of Flamingo Beach must have tuned in tonight. Some had opposing views but the discussion was lively, controversial, and at times irreverent, just like Tre liked it. Four hours would pass quickly tonight.

Jen stepped out of the shower, grabbed a towel and wrapped it around her dripping body. When the phone rang she considered letting the machine pick up but at the last minute grabbed it.

"Hello?"

"Watcha doing?" Chere bellowed.

Ignoring the puddle beginning to form on the white tile floor, Jen responded, "Getting ready to head for the Pink Flamingo to grab something to eat."

"Want company?"

"What about Leon? I thought you two were joined at the hip."

Chere sucked her teeth. "Leon who?"

Clearly that diversion was over with. Chere sounded perfectly fine. She was one of the most resilient people Jen had ever met.

Balancing the receiver between ear and shoulder, Jen said, "Okay, give me the lowdown."

"Turn your radio on, girl. Tune into WARP. D'Dawg's dissing you."

"Is it some kind of wrestling station?"

"Nope. The DJ's supposed to be finer than The Rock. Alls I know is he sure as hell cracks me up."

Jen vaguely recalled hearing something about a controversial show modeled after the New Yorker, Howard Stern's, except a whole lot cleaner.

"The man is slamming our column and he's got the listeners calling you Dear Jemima and saying you're a bigot."

"Why am I a bigot?"

"Might have something to do with your using the word 'queer.' You don't look a thing like that fat turban-headed woman selling her maple syrup."

Chere cracked her up. "Queer is politically correct," Jen explained. "I meant no disrespect. It's like the way colored evolved to Negro, then became black, and now African-American."

Her assistant snorted and began snapping her gum; at least Jen hoped that was what she was snapping. She refused to get bent out of shape. Controversy was her middle name.

"I'll turn on my radio and see what the fuss is about." Jen sighed. "All of that free advertising's bound to snag me more readers."

Snap. Snap. Snap. "And you'll take me on one ah dem 'Fun Ship' cruises?"

Jen's laughter rippled out. Chere supposedly had been the publisher, Ian Pendergrass's housekeeper. He'd had a one-night stand with her and to shut her up he'd given her a job.

"Here's the deal," Jen said, still laughing. "You read the mail when it comes in and keep me up to date, then we'll talk."

There wasn't a prayer in hell of Chere catching her up. She wasn't one to work harder than she needed to.

"Done. Tomorrow I'm going shopping for one ah them skimpy little bikinis that shows off my curves."

Jen wisely let that thread of conversation drop. Full-figured Chere in an itsy-bitsy bikini wasn't something she wanted to think about.

"See you at the Pink Flamingo in half an hour then," Jen said fumbling with the radio dial. She located WARP where a lively discussion was underway.

"Mama needs a good whopping," a strident male voice said. "Mabel shouldn't even be meddling in her grown son's affairs. And that advice columnist don't have a clue. Do you know the kind of women answering those personal ads?" The caller didn't wait for the DJ to comment. "Chicks no one else wants. Two tons of fun, and a whole lot neurotic."

The disk jockey chuckled. "I hear you. My man speaks from experience. Who in the house has been on one of those Internet dates? Step up now. Tell us if our man here is right."

Phones began ringing off the hook. It still amazed Jen just how much information people were willing to share about the intimate details of their lives. D'Dawg's audience for the most part were very vocal about her usage of the word *queer.*

The discord caused Jen to second-guess herself. Maybe as some had suggested she really should have told the old lady to get a life. Perhaps she could have presented other options, but she'd gone with her gut. And her gut seldom let her down.

D'Dawg's urban drawl snapped Jen back to the present.

"Any of you see *Dear Jenna* up close and personal? There's a photo in the newspaper with girl-friend wearing this little business suit, pearls and glasses. Looks to me like she stepped right outta the fifties. Uptight I say, lady needs a good loving to loosen her up."

The DJ's raucous laughter caused Jen to quickly shut off the radio. Even though only a chauvinist would have made that outrageous remark, he'd hit a nerve. Jen hadn't allowed a man to get next to her since Anderson dumped her. She was still recovering from his betrayal and it would be a cold day in hell before she trusted another man. She would play the same game men did. No connection and no commitment. Live in the present and enjoy each day as it came.

Jen had dated Anderson for two years. Even so, he'd walked away without an explanation and a short time later gotten engaged to another woman. Adding insult to injury, he'd purchased a home in the same Ashton suburb as Jen.

She would be late if she didn't hurry. Chere, the bottomless pit, would be waiting at the Pink Flamingo's bar checking out the prospects. After hurriedly zipping up the apricot sundress scooped low in the back, Jen stepped into matching wedge sandals. She finger-combed her shoulder-length hair and added a pair of gold hoop earrings. Convinced she no longer even faintly resembled *Dear Jenna,* she headed off.

Ten minutes later, Jen strolled into the packed Pink Flamingo. The place was filled with patrons winding down from a stressful work week. At the bar, groups of men nursed beers while female companions sipped on Cosmos and Appletinis. How could anyone possibly hear themselves? Jen wondered.

An olive-skinned hostess in a Flamingo Pink minidress chatted with a man Jen guessed to be the restaurant manager. He wore the exact color shirt. She tore herself away to point out a vacant seat at the outdoor bar.

Jen's first impressions were of Flamingo heaven or maybe it was hell. Fluttering from the thatched ceiling of the Tikki Hut were the pink birds in abundance. Jen eased onto the vacant bar stool, noting there was no sign of Chere. Her administrative assistant wasn't amongst the chattering twosomes and single hopefuls. Nor was she holding court with the two men at the end of the bar looking for action. The lighter one in a turquoise linen shirt, winked at Jen. Forcing herself, she winked back. She'd promised herself a new life.

Just then Chere entered in a ridiculously short skirt she had no business being in. Her cropped top exposed a layer of jiggling mahogany flesh. Two hundred pounds of confidence tottered across the floor in acrylic platform-soled sandals; a red hibiscus wobbled from the big toe.

"Sorry. Something came up," she said wedging herself between Jen and the man to her right.

Better not ask Chere what that might be, lest Chere told her.

Chere began flirting outrageously with the buff bartender.

"I'll have a glass of Chablis," Jen quickly interjected before things got out of hand.

"Make mine Sex on the Beach, Dwayne," Chere added coyly.

"Sure you don't want a Slow Comfortable Screw?"

While Jen sipped her wine, Chere stirred her drink with one finger and filled the bartender in on her issues with Leon. The two probably had history.

A bunch of nubile women were being checked out by the man who'd winked at Jen. On the rattan chairs, hopeful couples, many of the same gender, played footsie while sipping their drinks. Those more enterprising gyrated to the lively reggae band on the beach.

The decor was tropical, cheesy and in an odd way attractive. In the world Jen had left behind, people would be huddled in their winter coats dreaming about taking a trip to Florida.

A tall, well-built man in his late thirties climbed onto a vacated bar stool and ordered a gin and tonic. Although he eyed Jen, Chere slid her stool closer.

"Who's your friend?" he asked.

Chere sighed. "I'll introduce you, Quentin." She leaned suggestively against his arm as she made the introduction. "This here's Jen."

"I'm Quen Abrahams. The health club manager." He captured Jen's hand.

No wonder he was in such good shape. He got paid to work out.

"Nice to meet you."

"New to the area?"

"I've been here going on two months."

A loud female voice shouted, "Quen," and the man turned his attention to the new arrival.

The volume in the bar had risen. Chere left to make the rounds and Jen gave up on a sit-down meal and settled for a lobster sandwich.

When the band took a break someone turned up the stereo.

"If you're listening, dearie, I'm challenging you to hook up with me on the show."

There was that obnoxious DJ, again.

"Defend your position. Keep that radio tuned to WARP and find out if the lady can take the heat. I'm turning in for the night. Drive safely y'all, and remember WARP is the place to be."

Reminding herself no one in the place knew who she was, Jen checked the crowd's reaction. The few who were listening seemed mildly amused. It would be a cold day in hell before she accepted that Dog's challenge.

Chere was too busy chatting up a guy—who looked as if he might fall over if she bumped into him—to have heard the commentator. The man wore a thick gold chain around his neck and waved a fistful of bills at the bartender.

A smart woman would make her exit right now.

"Compliments of that gentleman," the bartender said, plopping a glass of wine in front of Jen, and rolling his eyes in the direction of a man with a Fu-Manchu rimming his lips.

Jen, about to protest, thought better of it. Her benefactor wasn't physically her type, but accepting a drink was not a lifetime commitment.

"Thank him for me," she said.

No sooner had she said that than the dark-skinned man with the mustache descended.

"Hi, hon, I'm Vince. I live in the villas across the street."

"Thanks again for the drink." She took a sip of wine to show her appreciation. "Sorry, I have to go. I'm working tomorrow." She slid off the stool, paid her bill and pocketed the business card Vince tucked into her hand.

Jen waved at him from the door. Chere was in a corner with the reed-thin guy. He had his arm around her. Maybe she'd better not leave her alone.

Reminding herself this wasn't Ashton, Ohio, where the sidewalk rolled up at midnight, Jen retraced her steps and headed back to rescue Chere.

Chapter 3

What seemed hours later, Jen entered the deserted lobby of Flamingo Place. A sleepy-eyed guard barely looked up as she hopped on the elevator. She got off at five and made her way down the hallway, almost running into a woman who looked to be no more than a teenager. She was exiting 5B. The child-woman clutched a collection of CDs. Her eyes brimmed over with tears.

Jen was tempted to offer a comforting shoulder but thought better of it. It wasn't her business. She continued on her way. But Tre's raucous music taunted her, following her to her apartment door. Was she the only person who objected to the assault on her ears? Her neighbors didn't seem to mind or didn't care to do anything about it. Maybe once she closed her door the commotion would cease.

But the tunes followed her into her apartment and continued even after she was ready for bed. Bleary-eyed, and knowing that she had to get up at six, she decided enough was enough.

Jen stomped to the phone. It was a waste of time calling Trestin whatever-his-name-was, even if she did know his last name. Time to go over his head. She punched in the numbers.

"Security?"

"Yes, ma'am."

"I'm calling from the fifth floor. 5B is keeping everyone up with his music."

"I'll see what I can do."

"I'd appreciate that." Jen disconnected the call.

Punching her pillow as if it were Trestin's handsome ebony face, she flopped back on the bed and tried closing her eyes. Maybe visualizing a day at the spa would help. But the image filling her vision was one of a dark-skinned broad-shouldered male well over six feet, with sculptured features and seductive bedroom eyes.

Ba dam, ba dam, ba dam. The music continued for another half hour and showed no signs of stopping. Calling security had been a waste of time.

Tomorrow she would go to the leasing office and lodge a formal complaint against Trestin Noisemaker. He'd pushed every hot button. Now it was war.

"Dammit!" Tre muttered, pounding the steering wheel of his silver Porsche. He spat out another graphic expletive and threw the vehicle into Park, the motor still running. Hopping out of the car, the roaring in his ears signaled his blood pressure was dangerously high. He circled.

The navy-blue Mazda Miata had no business in his reserved parking spot. He paid a premium amount every month for a location close to the building. Tre counted to ten. Years ago he would have put a dent in the Miata's hood and maybe a dent in the driver. All those anger management classes had helped mellow him out. He now knew how to redirect his pent-up outrage.

After getting back into the Porsche, Tre angled the vehicle in such a manner it blocked in the Miata, then sat back to wait. Reaching into the glove compartment, he removed a demo CD and slipped it into the player. The music, amateurish as he expected it to be, would help pass the time until the driver showed up.

Tre sipped from the bottle of water in the center console. The singer's sultry voice reminded him of Sade. She was the best thing he'd heard in a long time. Curiosity prompted him to pick up the disk's cover and stare into a heart-shaped face with smoky eyes. She would be promotable and worth playing on the station tonight.

Five minutes grew into ten. Tre's blood pressure shot even higher. His entire body felt as if it was on fire. The air conditioner was functional and on full blast. What was taking the irresponsible tenant so long to get back to their car? He or she must know that this wasn't their parking space.

Spotting one of the khaki-clad security guards, he flagged him down.

"Tre," the guard gushed, openly awestruck he'd been singled out. "Great show last night."

"Thanks. You wouldn't happen to know whose Miata that is?"

"No. But I can call a tow truck and get it hauled out of there."

"Let's give it ten minutes, then you can do what you need to do."

An SUV pulled up alongside them. Camille Lewis

hung out the window. "Tre," she said in her heavily accented voice, "what's with the Miata?" She peered at him over owl-like sunglasses.

Tre stretched his lips into a grimace of a smile. Camille was probably taking notes so that she could fill the building in. Now she stuck her entire head out of the window.

Tre tried to keep his voice even. "I guess someone decided my spot was more convenient than theirs."

"You know that someone," Camille said sweetly. "I'm going up. Want me to knock on 5C's door?"

"Please."

He was starting to lose it. Just this morning he'd gotten a call from the leasing office telling him they'd received a complaint about his loud music. It hadn't taken a rocket scientist to figure out who'd complained about him. He'd lived in the building over two years and not once had a neighbor ever called the leasing office on him. He'd planned on visiting the witch next door later and straightening her out. Now it looked like later was here.

"Should I call the tow truck?" the guard, whose head ping-ponged back and forth taking in the conversation, asked.

"No, hold off for a moment." Tre tossed the man a couple of CDs from his stash.

After thanking Tre profusely, the guard loped off. He yelled over his shoulder, "You're the man. Call the office if you need me, and I'll be here on the double."

Meanwhile Camille had parked her truck in the underground garage. She was undulating toward the building. Tre propped his feet on the console and prepared for a fight.

Ten minutes later, his attractive neighbor waltzed out. She had the grace to look embarrassed.

"I'm sorry, I didn't expect you'd come back so soon," she said, the moment he depressed the button and the window slid down. "I expected to be gone just a short time but then my phone rang."

He wanted to say, "You are so full of it." Angry as she'd made him, Tre couldn't help noticing the way the pencil-thin skirt with the slit cut high on the thigh hugged her hips, and those marvelous honey-colored thighs.

Sliding out of his vehicle, he rested his butt against the driver's door, crossed his arms, and gave Jen a steely-eyed look.

"You are probably one of the nerviest people I know. You called the leasing company on me, yet you have the gall to pull into a spot that costs money and isn't your own."

"It was close," Jen said disarmingly. "Was that

your music keeping me up all night or was that my imagination?"

Tre glared at her, ignoring the delicious smell of her perfume wafting his way. "What did you hope to accomplish by calling the leasing office?"

"I needed leverage to get through to you. I'd already tried appealing to your sense of decency."

He wanted to shake her. The truth was that he was actually enjoying the banter. His adrenaline flowed when a woman could keep up with him. And she wasn't starstruck. Maybe she didn't know who he was or simply didn't care. And even if she did, he had the feeling that his near celebrity status would not have made a difference.

"Truce?" Jen said, sticking out her hand. "Let me buy you lunch?"

He looked at her, frowning. This was one chick with lightning-quick moods. Just when he thought he'd figured her out.

"Fine and on one condition. No yogurt, rabbit food or cottage cheese for me. I'm not on a diet."

Tre allowed his eyes to travel the length of her body. His intent was to unnerve her. She didn't flinch.

Jen placed a hand on her hip as he continued to gawk. "Who said anything about being on a diet? Can you move your car so that I can get out? I'll check in

with you—maybe we can do that lunch later this
week. Now I have to go. I'm already late getting back
to work."

Move his car? She was in his spot.

"What is it you do that requires such dedication?"

She smiled. "Nothing important. Office work.
There's the usual hour for lunch and right now that
hour is up."

Tre sensed something missing. He didn't think
she was a clerk. She seemed too take-charge. She was
used to managing people. He got back in his car, and
slowly put the Porsche in Reverse.

Jen scooted into her vehicle and shouted from the
open window, "I'll be in touch." Burning rubber, she
zoomed from the parking lot.

Tre heard laughter drift from up above. Camille
was hanging out of her window, her cell phone to her
ear, watching as he maneuvered his car into the
vacant spot.

Jen St. George was a pain in the butt, and a fine-
looking pain at that. It would be his mission to get to
know her a whole lot better. She would be his challenge, a project to keep his adrenaline flowing.

Jen raced into her office waving a manila envelope
at Chere. "Got it!"

Flopping into her seat, she shoved the disk into the

computer's drive and began banging away at the keyboard. So much to do and so little time.

"Glad you found it," Chere said, looking up. "I wouldn't want to be around if you had to retype that whole thing."

Chere was actually attacking the stack in Jen's in-box. Visions of a cruise must be dancing in her head. Jen had raced home because she thought she'd misplaced the column she'd been working on practically all night.

"I worked on this thing, tweaking it until I was bleary-eyed. I didn't want to have to start again from scratch."

"Luis is looking for you," Chere muttered, a pen held between her clenched teeth. "Says it's important."

"Do you know what he wants?"

Since Jen started work at *The Chronicle,* Luis Gomez, her boss, had been too busy to do more than grunt in her direction. A compliment from him had been out of the question.

Jen reluctantly slid her chair out. She glanced at the sentences that Chere was highlighting.

Advice columnists are supposed to be open-minded.

Yet another reader ticked off at *Dear Jenna.*

"Who knows what Luis wants," Chere snorted. "My girls think something heavy's brewing. Maybe he's under pressure from the publisher because of all that squawking about you using the word *queer.*"

Jen groaned. "This is getting old. I'll go see what Luis wants."

Jen wended her way through a maze of cubicles, passing other staff members absorbed in various stages of production. Heads shot up as she went by but things seemed quiet, too quiet. She'd learned to pay attention to her instincts and something was definitely brewing. She had the unsettling feeling everyone knew she had an audience with Luis.

Luis Gomez was sprawled behind the cluttered desk of his enormous corner office. A huge glass wall provided him with an unobstructed view of the newsroom. The room was poorly lit. Luis depended on his desk lamp to read. He was huddled over, squinting at some piece of copy and she couldn't make out his expression. His office was called The Dungeon, and for good reason.

"You wanted to see me?" she asked from the doorway.

Luis had an unlit cigar clamped between his yellowing teeth. The half-moon glasses perched on the end of the nose gave him a mad scientist look. Totally ignoring the smoke-free environment, he'd clearly had a few drags. Jen had never seen Luis light up, but his office smelled like an ashtray and the odor lingered around him. He waved a meaty paw, gesturing for her to come in.

"Grab a seat," he said, poking a stubby finger at a chair filled with newspapers.

Jen scooped the papers up but kept standing. There was no place to put them, at least no place she saw.

"Lay the lot over here." Luis made room for the pile by sweeping another stack of newspapers to the floor. "Take a load off."

Jen finally slid into the chair directly facing him.

"We got problems. We need to fix them," Luis barked.

"What kinds of problems?" Jen asked carefully.

"Flamingo Beach is all stirred up. The gay alliance is bitching up a storm, claiming you're homophobic."

"Why?"

"Let me spell it out," Luis said, enunciating his words. "There is a very vocal leader who wants your hide. They're ticked off and feel that you're prejudiced against gays."

Jen was out the chair like a shot. "That's ridiculous. 'Queer' is a current-day expression."

"Our readership is diverse," Luis said patiently.

"This is a conservative town, but our gay alliance is powerful. We need to stay on their good side."

"I see."

Luis Gomez just reinforced everything she'd suspected. He was a wuss.

"I want you to use the Sunday column to publish a retraction."

"You want me to placate the group?"

"Do what you need to do. But when you write this Sunday's column make sure to stress you're in favor of alternative lifestyles. You may even want to state that your bachelor's mother needs to encourage open and honest communication with her son. Make sure to mention America is about freedom of choice."

"Will you be writing my column for me?" Jen inquired coolly. Why all of a sudden was Luis pandering to a group he'd never openly supported? She'd privately thought him to be homophobic.

"Not writing, just suggesting. I've lived in this town long enough to know the gay alliance can make things damn uncomfortable."

Luis crooked a finger, beckoning Jen closer.

Jen reluctantly took a couple of steps toward him then stopped. She thought she would gag from the smell of stale tobacco.

"The mayor's son, Chet, is gay," Luis confided.

"Now you don't want to tick off such an influential person. Solomon Rabinowitz may not be happy about his son's sexual preference, but blood rules in the long run. He'll support him and back the alliance one hundred percent."

Jen took a deep breath. Should she tell Luis? No it would be her ace card. She'd learned one thing during her years as an advice columnist though: once you started waffling, you cut your own throat. From then on anything you said would be challenged. Her instincts told her to stick to her guns. But common sense reminded her she was the newbie in town and still unproven.

"I'll compromise," Jen promised. "How about I publish letters with contradictory opinions from mine."

"Think about what I said," Luis said, picking up the phone and punching in numbers. "The paper's been flooded with calls. That disk jockey from WARP is all over you. He's even challenging you to come on his station."

"And maybe I will."

Luis's glasses slipped a notch. "I don't think I heard you correctly."

"Think ratings, Luis. Think of the papers we'd sell."

"Hmmmmm. I'll reserve commentary until I see this week's numbers."

"By the way, Luis," Jen said, preparing to leave. "My brother Ellis is queer."

Luis's lower lip flapped open. He quickly composed himself. "I want readers to love *Dear Jenna*," he said gruffly. "They should be hanging on to her every word. I'm grooming you to be the next Abby."

His phone rang. "Luis Gomez. Sure, I'll hold for the mayor."

Jen had thought Luis Gomez was a wuss. Now she knew he was just playing the political game.

Chapter 4

Tre held the receiver away from his ear. For the last three minutes the station's manager and owner had been yakking on and on, acting as if Tre was the best thing since pumpernickel.

Boris was an ex-army brat of bi-racial descent. He was the product of an African-American mother and a German father. The Germanic genes overrode the African. Boris was usually not this effusive. Something most definitely was up.

"Ratings are soaring. You've got Flamingo Beach hooked on WARP," Boris gushed.

Perhaps it was time to hit him up for a raise. No, he'd wait to do it face-to-face. Eyeball-to-eyeball.

"How about I come in a half an hour early before the show. We'll talk then."

"Wait! Wait!" Boris shouted. "We need more than a half an hour to formulate a plan. We need to keep this momentum going. Do what you need to do to get that columnist on the show. I'll make it worth your while."

"I'll see what I can do."

Tre hung up thinking that any hope of getting some shut-eye before his show was impossible now. What did Boris mean by he would make it worth his while? Did it mean that he would finally get the coveted prime-time slot and would have his own syndicated show? Or did it mean that there would be some money coming his way?

Either way, the conversation had left Tre wound up and wired. He paced the spacious living room, circled around the sectional couch and crossed over to the French doors that led out to a balcony with an unfettered view of the ocean. This was what living in Florida was all about. This was what he had worked for.

There was a certain tranquility that came with living on the water. He even loved the briny ocean smell. Maybe a run would loosen him up. No, he didn't have time to cover his usual five miles today. He would just have to stand here taking everything in, breathe and enjoy it.

Several industrious souls were taking advantage of the cooler temperatures. The boardwalk was busy for that time of day, probably because the sunset promised to be a beauty. Teenagers whizzed by on skateboards and Rollerblades, almost knocking the pedestrians over. A few senior citizens, those who'd stood their ground refusing to move when gentrification rolled around, carried groceries in the baskets of their three-wheel bikes. Much as Tre sometimes groused about Flamingo Beach's lack of sophistication, he had to admit he had it made.

He thought about earlier today when he'd allowed Jen St. George to push his buttons. He'd worked damn hard on controlling a temper that had often gotten him in trouble and he wasn't going to let the ballsy woman undo all of his hard work.

He ran a hand over the closely cropped hair that his fans, mostly female, said made him look sexy and mysterious. They compared him to supermodel Ty Beckford. Must be the dark, shiny skin. Lines like that had once fed his ego. But his days of quick hits and meaningless sex were over with. He was looking

for something more substantial now. Maybe even
marriage, but something longer lasting than the oc-
casional fling.

Thoughts of sex made Jen St. George come to
mind. Now she would be a woman he wouldn't mind
breaking his forced celibacy for. She intrigued him
because she was not impressed or intimidated by
him. He'd have to make sure he took her up on her
lunch invitation and soon.

Right now he had a bigger challenge; how to get
that *Dear Jenna* woman on his show. Ratings were
everything. Ratings were what Boris understood. If
he could persuade her to have a live debate he'd have
it made. He'd get her on the air and make mincemeat
of her. *Dear Jenna* could help get him where he
needed to go.

He definitely had big plans for himself. One of
them was moving up to an urban city where his hip
way of talking and crass irreverence would be applauded and not misunderstood, where he would
reach a bigger audience that was not necessarily
white or black. He needed a major radio station that
would recognize his talent and reward it accordingly.

Tre planned on holding his own with the likes of
Howard Stern. A Northeast audience would get him.
They were usually sophisticated and more worldly.

His voice could reach millions and not just the thousands it did today.

He imagined the rush of walking down the street and having people stop him to shake hands or maybe they'd just reach out to touch him. He would be an inspiration to his people, especially little black boys who'd strayed. He'd been kind of wayward himself growing up. Yes, New York City would be part of the plan. It was not an impossible goal if he played his cards right.

As Tre continued to fantasize about New York City and a growing fan base his eyelids grew heavy. He jolted awake at the sound of the alarm clock that luckily he'd remembered to set earlier on.

Jen had just gotten out of the shower and was wrapping her body in a fluffy towel when the doorbell rang. It played one of her favorite tunes. Jen groaned. Hopefully security would have called before letting Chere up.

The bell rang again. It sounded like her visitor had put an index finger to the spot and forgotten it. Fine, she wasn't going to be given much of a choice. Her robe, the one she hadn't worn in years, was still in a box in her closet. Whoever it was would have to deal with her the way she was.

She took her time getting to the front door, and took another second pressing her eye to the peephole. She assessed the distorted image, trying to determine whether it was male or female.

Trestin Noisemaker had come to her. She hadn't had to make that phone call to invite him to lunch. Jen made sure the bath towel was tightly tucked around her before opening the door a crack.

"Yes?"

"Can I come in?"

"No you may not. To what do I owe this pleasure?"

"I came with a peace offering."

"I invited you to lunch," she tossed back. "That was my peace offering for parking in your spot."

An arm thrust through the opening, holding something in a tissue wrapper.

"Uh-uh!" Jen said, closing the door an inch on that arm.

"It's wine. Try it, you'll like it," Trestin sang.

"I can't accept it."

"Why not?"

She thought for a moment, her front teeth clamped down on her bottom lip. "Because, well because, I don't accept gifts from men."

"I'm not just any man. I'm your neighbor. I've kept you up at night. This is my way of saying I'm sorry."

Camille Lewis probably had an eye to the peephole. Most likely so did Ida. The entire building could be listening to her business.

"Can't I come in for a minute?" Tre whined.

"I'm not dressed." One hand gripped the top of the towel even as she stood aside, allowing him to enter.

Trestin placed one foot on the threshold, the other in the hallway. He was still holding the wine.

"I've never been accused of forcing myself on a woman," he said, smiling at her unease.

"There's always a first time."

Trestin's gaze swept over the living and dining space. "Nice place."

"Thanks."

Jen took the wine bottle from him and set it down on her sideboard.

"It's a lovely cabernet," Tre added. "Perhaps you can save it for when we have dinner."

"In that case it might turn to vinegar. We are having lunch, not dinner," she reminded him.

"Look," Tre said, "I don't have the time or inclination to turn this into a pissing contest. I'm on my way to work. Drink it alone and in good health."

"I'll accept your gift on one condition," she surprised herself by saying.

He hiked an eyebrow. "And that is?"

"We have our drink in public. And by that I don't mean a cozy restaurant."

"Where did you have in mind?"

"Neutral territory. We take the bottle to the beach or around the pool. Somewhere on the property where everyone can see us."

"I'll accept your invitation on one condition," he now countered.

"And what is that?"

"You wear your sexiest bathing suit to the pool. While you think about that, I have to go."

"What is it that you do?" Jen called to his disappearing back.

"Let's just say I'm in communications," he tossed over his shoulder.

"So am I."

The moment she shut the door she marched over to where she'd set the bottle down. Curious to see if his taste matched hers, Jen removed the bottle of wine from its wrapper and checked out the label. The wine had to have set him back at least a twenty spot.

The annoying man actually had good taste.

Boris Schwartz, WARP's owner and station manager, was seated in his office, a cooling mug of coffee in front of him as usual. Tre leaned his butt against the doorjamb, fingered the diamond stud in his ear, and waited for Boris to look up.

"You're ten minutes late," he announced, glancing up and beckoning Tre to come in.

"Sorry. I got held up."

"Hmmmm."

"You said you wanted to talk to me."

"Have a seat."

"I prefer to stand."

"Suit yourself."

The Afro-German brought the mug to his lips. His eyes never left Tre's. In one precise movement, he set the cup down on a desk that was painfully neat. "Get *Dear Jenna* on your show while the interest level is still there. It should happen in the next day or two. Understand?"

Tre felt like clicking his heels and saying "Aye, aye, sir." Instead he said, "And if the woman won't agree to come on?"

"Appeal to her ego. There's something in this for both of you." Boris's index finger made a *rat-a-tat* sound on his desk. "There's got to be some kind of carrot we can dangle to get her on WARP."

"I have an idea," Tre said, a smile creeping across his face. It was raw and unformed but it just might work. "I'll call Chet Rabinowitz."

"The mayor's son? The leader of the gay coalition or alliance or whatever it's called."

"Alliance. He's an acquaintance of mine."

Boris scrunched a nose that took up the majority of his face. "Where are you going with this?"

"Tell me what I can expect if these ratings continue the way they've been lately, and I'll share with you what I have in mind."

"You drive a hard bargain."

For the next fifteen minutes Boris spoke and Tre listened, interrupting occasionally to get specifics when he felt he might be getting snowed.

Tre left the station manager's office feeling upbeat and positive. He was well on his way.

Now to get Chet Rabinowitz to agree to come on the air. If he dangled the promise of an on-air discussion of the *Dear Jenna* column, that might persuade the vocal activist to say yes. Chet was a publicity hound, especially if it would further the gay cause.

And, if these broadcasts went as Tre thought they would, D'Dawg would then invite Daddy, the mayor, to come on the show.

Tre rubbed his hands together gleefully. Yes! He was onto something. He was on a roll.

* * *

Chet Rabinowitz was with a customer when the phone rang. His partner Harley hurried off to get it. Business had been slow lately and they needed a large order to help pay this month's expenses.

"All About Flowers," Harley, the alpha part of the twosome answered in his low baritone. "It's for you, Chet," he said, waving the phone at him.

Chet hurried to take the call, leaving Rico Catalban still debating over what color roses to send to his newly hired hostess at the Pink Flamingo. In a small town like Flamingo Beach where everyone knew each other, no employee would dare file sexual harassment charges if the romantic interest wasn't reciprocated. Not if they knew what was good for them. They'd be laughed off the beach and most certainly would not be hired by any other local merchant, not even for a menial job.

"This is Chet," the florist gushed.

Music played in the background but no one responded. Chet frowned. It was probably a solicitor, but maybe not—Harley would have hung up on her.

Chet covered the mouthpiece with his hand. "Who's looking for me?"

Harley shrugged. "I don't know. The person was

well spoken. I thought it might be a reporter. We did send out that press release."

Harley continued to make suggestions to the Catalban man, who was beautiful enough to be a woman, before he finally shouted over his shoulder, "On second thought, it might be the radio station. I think I heard WARP mentioned and that DJ with the canine name."

"Oh!" Chet's Kenneth Cole loafers now tapped out a beat. He'd had a secret crush on Tre Monroe. Too bad the DJ wasn't into men. One perfectly manicured finger worried his long lashes. It felt wonderful to be fully out of the closet and able to openly admire someone of the same gender.

"D'Dawg calling for Charles Rabinowitz," a deep male voice said.

"This is Chet, Tre. Long time no talk?" Was he being too familiar? They were really only nodding acquaintances, though privately Chet thought the African-American man was the buffest male he knew and the hottest. They worked out at the same health club. Tre's dark-skinned good looks, sculptured features and soulful brown eyes belonged on a male model. Too bad he hadn't chosen a profession where he could strut his stuff. He would have given Ty Beckford a run for his money.

"If I were any better, I would be purring," the sexy DJ said.

Chet loved the sound of his voice. It came from deep in his belly and reminded him of a popular R&B singer.

"Is there something that All About Flowers can do for you?" he asked.

Chet already had visions of gaining WARP's exclusive account, maybe even being put on a retainer. The free publicity would be just what the store needed and if Tre only mentioned the flower shop once on the show they'd have it made.

"What are you doing tomorrow night, say around nine?" Tre asked.

Chet laid an open palm on his chest where his heart was supposed to be. Using his other hand, he crooked a finger at his lover and inhaled loudly. But Harley was already on a roll, explaining to Rico that some women liked a more subtle approach. He was busy recommending flowers that were classy and understated, suggesting calla lilies, orchids or even sunflowers as alternatives. "Why be like any other chap on the make sending the usual boring dozen roses?" Chet heard Harley ask.

"What did you have in mind?" Chet countered, focusing on his caller again.

"Come be a guest on my show. You can plug your flower shop as much as you like."

"Why?"

Oh, my Gawd! This was a dream come true. It was an opportunity no one in his right mind would pass up!

"I'm interested in your reaction to *Dear Jenna*'s advice. I want to know what the community thinks of her using the word *queer.* And I want to know what your group would like to see happen."

"The word *queer* is—"

"Yeah, I know. Offensive. You're gay. You've worked hard to earn respect. You enjoy an alternative lifestyle. Use my show to straighten out the lady. She's new in town. We can't allow some upstart to get away with offending upstanding citizens."

"Good point!" Chet was swept along with the excitement. Being asked on the D'Dawg show was an honor. He would be a fool to miss out on the opportunity to increase business for the flower shop.

He got the particulars and hung up after agreeing to be at the station half an hour before the start of the show.

Now he needed to center himself. Chet hurried in the direction of the bathroom. When he returned, Harley had completed his sales pitch. Rico bought his suggestions and Harley wrapped the huge Vanda orchid in cellophane and added curled ribbons to the arrangement as a festive touch.

"There, Bianca will love it," Harley said. "If she doesn't she's not the woman for you."

Chet waited for Rico to leave the store before sinking onto the pink divan with the claw feet.

"I think I'm going to faint."

"Please don't. At least wait until we're sure no customers are around. I'll get you water and a cold cloth for your beet-red face."

"I'm hyperventilating," Chet said, now prostrate on the seat.

Harley was back with a chilled bottle of water. "Here, take deep breaths. What did Tre Monroe want with you?"

Chet fanned his heated cheeks with his open palm. "He asked me on the show. Me, Harley. He wanted my opinion on missy, you know that Jenna woman, the advice columnist."

"You don't say. Work it, boy. This is a good opportunity to promote All About Flowers."

"So you approve? You think I should go?"

"Of course. You'll be supported by every gay person in this town. Your appearing on the show will increase our visibility and will let these uptight folks know that we are a force to be reckoned with."

Harley's fingers cupped Chet's chin. "You don't think you're being set up, do you?"

Chet frowned. He hadn't thought of that possibility. "What would be the point? Tre is not a stupid man. He knows who my father is. While Dad may not agree with my choices he would never publicly say it. He would defend me to the core. We are after all part of his constitution. My mother would leave him if he turned against me, his own child."

"Okay, if you say so, but I smell a rat. You know what I think?" Harley didn't wait for an answer. "I think he's also invited Dear Jenna on the show."

"No, he didn't."

"I bet you dinner he did."

Chapter 5

"It's for you," Chere said, waving the phone at Jen. Her voice was loud enough that many of the staff in the surrounding cubicles stuck their heads over the partitions.

Jen, busily banging away, was more preoccupied with meeting the deadline for this Sunday's paper than taking calls from Flamingo Beach's ticked citizens. Words were not coming easily today, largely because she was censoring herself. She'd never had to pick and choose her words before. Now because of that disconcerting conversation with Luis she was being careful.

She looked up, pen clenched between her teeth and said, "Find out who it is and take a message."

"Maybe you don't want to do that."

"Why not?"

Chere came closer, one large hand clamped over the mouthpiece. "It sounds important."

Exasperated, Jen huffed out a sigh. "Whatever. Deal with it, Chere. Just take a message and I'll return the call."

Trestin had beaten her to it. He'd taken the initiative to invite her to lunch today. She'd accepted only because she felt guilty. With a tight deadline hovering, she should have pushed him off until the following week. But he'd been both insistent and persistent. He'd even stopped by her apartment again.

Thankfully she'd been out, so he'd slid a note under her door. Jen's guilt had kicked in. She'd felt obligated to accept. She was the one who'd initially offered. She'd go just to keep the peace. After all, she lived next door to the man. It might pay to be civil.

Chere returned the receiver to her ear. She fumbled for her high school English. "*Dear Jenna* isn't here. Who'd you say this is again? Oh, my God! You gotta be kidding. What does he want with *Dear Jenna?*" Picking up a pencil, she began scribbling, then shoved the note in Jen's direction. "Sure you don't want to pick up. No not you," she said back into the receiver. Chere was breathing heavily when she hung up.

"That phone call has you that worked up?" Jen said, her fingers flying.

"That was that DJ from WARP. He wants you to come on the show." Chere was now hopping up and down on those ridiculous platform heels, double chins bouncing. Every piece of loose flesh jiggling.

The pen Jen still clenched between her teeth, escaped her grip, falling on the Formica desk and rolling across the floor.

"Why would he think I'd want to be on his show?"

Chere's massive quarterback's shoulders rose. "Luis would want you to step up to the challenge. You said you were interested in growing readership. This is one way to do it. I'm so excited I have to go to the loo." She tottered from the room and headed for the bathroom. Jen suspected she was off to fill in her buddies who made up most of the clerical staff.

Chere was back in twenty minutes huffing and puffing. "You betcha call that radio station," she threatened.

Jen rolled her eyes. "Don't hold your breath."

"You have to," Chere said advancing. "My girls

listen to WARP all day long. Tonight's broadcast is hot. They got the mayor's son coming to talk about you."

"They do not. And even if they did I'm not being baited into responding." Jen's attention returned to her column. She muttered, "The mayor's son can get on the radio and say whatever he wants. If I leave it alone and not take a defensive mode this whole thing will eventually blow over."

"That's what you think." Chere snorted. "You haven't lived in this town long enough."

Jen glanced at her watch. If she didn't leave right away she would be late for her lunch appointment. She'd insisted she make the reservations. She'd chosen home turf. They would be lunching at the Pink Flamingo restaurant. Out in the open and rela- tively safe.

"Save whatever else you have to say for later. I have to go," Jen said, picking up her purse. "Make sure to answer the phones."

Chere mumbled something under her breath. It was probably a good thing Jen didn't hear.

Fifteen minutes later she hurried into the Pink Flamingo. Considering it was a weekday, it was crowded. The same hostess from the other night seated her. Today she wore a flamingo pink miniskirt and midriff-baring top. No sign of Trestin as yet. Jen followed the curvaceous young woman to a table in the center of the room, noticing the small butterfly tattooed on her lower back.

Ten minutes, and two glasses of water later, Jen was still waiting for her next-door neighbor to show up. Fifteen minutes later she was still waiting. Left with nothing else to do but people-watch, her eyes focused on the Pepto-Bismol pink walls and the fluttering flamingos. The décor in this part of the room had a distinctly beachy flavor to it. Old fishermen's nets were artfully draped on the walls, filled with starfish, fake lobsters and other types of crustacean.

It was an interesting assortment of people gathered. There were a few from the complex Jen had a nodding acquaintance with, but the majority she didn't recognize. She did spot Camille Lewis, the woman who lived on her floor, seated across from a pleasant-looking bald man who couldn't seem to get a word in edgewise.

Jen also spotted Quen Abrahams, the health club manager with a blonde who looked like she might be someone he personally trained. There were business types, judging by their attire, huddled in a corner conducting a meeting, and a handful of sleek ladies with big hair who looked like they did lunch for a living.

Waiting was getting old and she had too much to do.

She'd give Trestin another five minutes and then she was out of here. He'd proven to be an inconsiderate person anyway, so it was no surprise if he stood her up.

Jen sipped her water and decided her energy was best channeled elsewhere. She should never have invited Trestin to lunch in the first place. Her peace offering was not appreciated. Taking her purse with her, she slid from the booth.

"Where do you think you're going?" a deep, male voice with a timbre that actually made her shiver said. Jen's lunch partner grasped her elbow.

She schooled herself not to react. "You're late. I didn't think you were showing up."

Trestin looked cool, composed and strikingly handsome. He was wearing a beige linen shirt and black drawstring pants; the eighty-degree-plus weather outside was having no apparent effect on him. He made Jen feel wilted and wrinkled in the cotton sundress she'd chosen because it didn't require ironing.

"I was held up because someone parked in my spot," Tre said smoothly. "More time was wasted trying to get hold of the towing service. You should understand."

"Not again." The words slipped out before she could censor them.

Trestin's index finger stabbed the air. "Gotcha."

"You…" Jen sputtered.

Trestin roared. Jen got a good glimpse of strong white teeth and healthy gums.

He was by far the most cocky and irreverent person she'd ever met. A while back he'd mentioned something about being in communications. Jen wondered what exactly that meant. She waited until they were seated and the waiter had taken their orders to ask.

"You said you were in communications. What does that mean?"

"Just that. I'm very good at what I do. That's enough about me. Let me take a guess at what you do."

Jen felt some trepidation build. Being in the advice business came with an awful stigma. Not that she particularly cared how she was perceived by him. But she did want to guard her privacy. It was better to be faceless when you did what she did.

"Hold on to that thought. Here comes our food," she said. "We have to eat quickly—my lunchtime's almost up." What she didn't say was that she'd allotted two hours to make this lunch happen.

They dug into their respective meals. Jen had chosen lobster salad, because she couldn't afford another pound on her hips and Trestin had ordered scallops on a bed of greens with sliced avocado on the side. They sipped sparkling water.

"Back to our original conversation," Trestin said. "You're an attorney."

"Not exactly."

"A doctor?"

She shook her head. "You're way off base." She was starting to enjoy this.

"You're a professional of some sort. I can tell from the way you speak, hold yourself. You have this inner confidence. You could be a teacher although I don't think so. Maybe you're the principal of a high school."

"Wrong on all counts."

"Tell me."

"You're the one that wanted to take a shot at it."

Silence descended as they returned to their entrées. Trestin ate with a certain amount of relish while Jen, conscious of the passing time, scarfed down the remainder of her lobster salad.

They were almost through with the meal when Camille and the man Jen assumed was her husband arrived.

Trestin brought the napkin to his lips. "Hello, Winston, Camille." He nodded at the couple. "Good to see you."

"That was one brilliant move," Winston said. "I'm looking forward—"

"You haven't met Jen." She was quickly introduced. Trestin flashed the older man a look Jen wasn't sure how to interpret.

"I'm looking forward to tonight," Winston said, his hand on his wife's arm. "We wouldn't disturb you further."

Camille who'd so far remained mercifully quiet didn't budge.

"You two have something going?" she asked boldly.

"Camille!" Winston sounded outraged. He was clearly the classier half. "Check yourself."

"I am checking myself. I'm not going behind their backs. I'm asking them directly. Now I know why you were parked in his spot." She eyed Jen knowingly.

Should she straighten the nosy woman out? No, that type of personality would believe what they wanted to believe.

"Come on, Camille," Winston said, attempting to leave again.

"*Dear Jenna'*s up next," Camille said, wagging a finger at Trestin. "I just know it."

Winston tugged on his wife's arm and they finally left.

After they were out of earshot, Jen said, "What's this about *Dear Jenna?*"

"Nothing for you to worry your pretty little head about."

She hated to be dismissed or patronized. He'd been pleasant company so far and he'd kept her entertained. They'd even managed not to insult each other. But Trestin was ruining it all by being dismissive. She hated when men did that to women, acting like they didn't have a right to question them.

Jen signaled to the waiter for the check.

"It's been taken care of," Tre announced, stopping the man from coming over with a shake of his head.

"When? Why?"

"Because I wanted to and I have an open tab here. I arranged it on my way in."

Jen searched through her purse. "I promised you lunch. I'm paying. It was my way of apologizing to you for being inconsiderate."

"Apology accepted. You can pay for dinner this Saturday night?"

"What?" He was asking her out. She should be flattered. She could do far worse than this man with his to-die-for good looks. Admittedly in some bizarre way she was attracted to him. But he lived next door and if it didn't work out things would be awkward. Better to keep things on a neighborly basis.

"Lunch has been great. I enjoyed it," Jen said honestly. "But Saturday night is out of the question. I'm on a tight deadline and will probably be working."

"You never did say what it is you did."

By divine intervention, Jen's cell phone rang. She glanced at the screen, recognizing her own office number.

"Chere?"

"Yes, child. Luis is looking for you. You need to get back here on the double."

"What's wrong? Everyone that needed to know knew I had plans for an extended lunch."

Jen glanced up to see Trestin's arched eyebrows.

"Problem?" he mouthed.

She shook her head. "I'm on my way." Jen tucked the flip phone back into her purse. "Thanks for lunch," she said to Trestin. "Now I really have to get going."

"I know," he shouted at her back when the valet brought the Miata around and she was stepping into it. "High-class call girl."

Jen took her time tipping the valet and putting the car into gear. She slid the window down stuck her hand out and gave him the finger.

Chapter 6

On the drive back to the office, Jen thought about her ballsy neighbor. He really was like no one she'd ever met before. She'd revised her opinion of him. Sure, he came off as cocky, self-centered and more than a tad selfish, but he did have a wicked sense of humor and held his own with her. *Single-minded* would be the word she used to describe him.

Jen had decided that his being in "communications" meant he was a stand-up comic or possibly an actor. She also realized she didn't know what Trestin's last name was and had forgotten to ask.

Drat! She should have gotten a business card from him. Days ago she'd tried looking for a name on his mailbox, but like her, he'd requested the label be left blank.

After parking her car, she rushed into the building. Why was Luis so bent out of shape about her leaving the office? He'd never paid much attention to her comings and goings before. It wasn't like she'd just disappeared. She'd sent him an e-mail, copying the world that she would be taking an extended lunch.

Chere intercepted her on the way to see Luis. She waved fire-engine-red talons with rhinestones in a rainbow of colors, in the direction of their boss's office.

"They're in there. All the bigwigs. They've been at it a while."

Jen spotted Luis, assorted department heads, and a tall silver-haired man who looked like he was pushing eighty if he was a day, through Luis's glass walls.

"Who's he?" Jen asked, inclining her head slightly in the direction of where the men gathered.

"Ian Pendergrass, the publisher of *The Flamingo Chronicle*. My old man." Chere put a cupped hand to her mouth and pretended to cough. "My ex," she whispered.

So the rumors were true. Now was not the time to ask.

"Better go. They're waiting," Chere said.

What could this mean? Jen was still preoccupied when she entered Luis's office. It had to be big for all these busy people to stop everything they were doing and gather here. She couldn't imagine she was being fired. Luis would not need a committee present to say what he had to say.

"There you are," Luis greeted her as she stuck her head through the open doorway. "And about time." Noticeably absent was his unlit cigar. Ian Pendergrass was a man he either respected or feared. Luis waved her in.

The men stood as Jen entered. The sole woman stayed in her chair. "Did I miss a meeting?" Jen asked, her voice upbeat, her demeanor outwardly calm.

Luis cleared his throat. "Yes, you did. Have you met our publisher, Ian Pendergrass?"

He knew damn well she hadn't. Jen managed a smile as the old man enveloped her hand in a firm grip and held it a second longer than necessary.

"We meet at last," he said, his warm blue gaze sweeping over her. "I've heard quite a bit about you."

She bet he had.

Ian patted the vacant chair. "Sit."

As she did so the group resumed their animated discussion as if she didn't exist.

"It's a no-brainer. She's got to go on the show," Percy, the circulations manager said emphatically.

"And I say, she shouldn't. You'll be throwing her to the wolves and what good will that do?"

"Drive business for one. Have you seen our numbers? We're having the most profitable quarter in the history of *The Chronicle.*" This came from Percy again.

Jen stayed quiet and listened, trying to grasp what was going on. She was the topic of a heated discussion, that much she knew.

Pendergrass was up and pacing. Despite the high temperatures outside, his lanky frame was encased in a double-breasted blue jacket with the brass buttons buttoned. His light-gray slacks had sharp creases to them. And his tasseled loafers shone. Overall he looked polished and successful as if he'd just stepped off his yacht.

"Luis, we've been going round and round about this for some time and you haven't spoken up," he said.

Luis darted a look Jen's way. "Both arguments have merit," he said. "Jen's been working on the Sunday column. Our approach is to downplay what was said, maybe even admit we came on too strong."

She'd never actually agreed to that.

"Luis!"

He ignored her, continuing, "Then again, that radio DJ's pretty slick. Jen might get tricked into saying something she didn't mean."

Luis as usual was waffling.

"She's already used the word *queer*," Ian came back with. "As far as this town's concerned it doesn't get much worse than that." He chuckled.

"Wait! Wait! Wait!" Jen shouted, bolting to her feet. "Don't I have a say in any of this? Here you are making decisions for me as if I were an inanimate object."

"She is a pistol." Ian's smile was a mile wide. He crossed his arms. "Luis, since you're her boss. You should be the one to catch her up."

Luis Gomez spent another five minutes recounting what had transpired in the short time Jen was gone. The wisecracking WARP DJ had called around until he found someone willing to listen. Someone had put him through to Luis's office then tracked Ian Pendergrass down on his cell phone and that's how the impromptu meeting had come about.

"Why are we even entertaining me going on the show?" Jen said more quietly. "I shouldn't have to defend myself and *The Chronicle* shouldn't even dignify WARP by responding. Turn on the television and read any major magazine. Today, the gay population refers to themselves as queer. There's even a popular television show."

"I know," Luis said, his tone designed to smooth things over. "But this is a conservative paper and a conservative town. *The Chronicle*'s sales are up and we need to do whatever it takes to keep this paper selling."

Even if it meant using her as the sacrificial lamb. Luis really was a wuss straddling both sides of the fence.

"Yes, we do have to think about sales," Todd Hirsch, the director of multimedia and new projects interjected. "Distribution is at an all time high this week. *The Southern Tribune*'s watching us closely. They're scared to death—I even had one of their reporters in looking for a job. Change has been a long time coming to *The Flamingo Beach Chronicle*. The first step was hiring you. We've never had an advice columnist before. You've earned your salary and some. We've made news."

It was the first time Jen had received any acknowledgment that her contribution to the paper made a difference. Despite the unpleasant nature of the meeting it felt good to be publicly recognized.

Ian tapped the face of his watch. "We need to wrap this up. I have to go. Have we reached a consensus?"

"I say Jen goes on the show." This came from Todd.

"I say we don't bow to pressure," Eileen Brown, who headed up advertising, and was the only other woman in the room, added.

Jen had been introduced to Eileen briefly. She too was African-American. They'd never said more than "hi" to each other. Now Jen warmed to her, glad to have found a supportive friend amongst the crowd.

"She goes on," Percy said, giving the nod.

"No she doesn't."

And so it went. Finally Ian held his palms up. "Why don't we wait until after tonight's broadcast, then make a decision. Chet Rabinowitz could very well make an ass of himself and that will be the end of that."

"I doubt he will," Eileen said surprising them. Every head in the room now swiveled in her direction. "Chet is well-spoken and well-regarded and he is the politician's son. I've heard from a good source, his father, the mayor will be a guest on WARP the following night."

"Solomon Rabinowitz is a guest on the station?" Ian's facial expression registered incredulity. "The mayor's not exactly Baby Face or P. Diddy. He's hardly the type WARP has on. Aren't they more of an R&B or rap station?"

"The mayor will pander to any crowd at this point," Percy said sourly.

"Not just any crowd." This again came from Eileen. "He's looking for votes in the upcoming election. Chet is his son and Mayor Rabinowitz's appearance on the D'Dawg show will send a powerful message. Solomon's up for election in the next few months and he's shrewd enough to realize the opposition is young, popular and forward-thinking. The mayor may need the gay and African-American vote to win."

Everyone began talking at once as the news slowly sank in. When there was a lull in the conversation, all eyes were fixed on Luis.

He began to speak haltingly, "If Mayor Rabinowitz goes on WARP…uh, Jen will have to go on." Noting Jen's expression, he held a palm up like a traffic cop. "Not necessarily to defend yourself but to say exactly what you said to me. We might be able to turn this thing around and make the rabble-rousers look silly and uninformed. We can have PR coach you if necessary."

Jen exchanged a look with Eileen and shook her head.

Ian Pendergrass was pacing, but he slowed down to say, "I'm afraid Luis is right. Jen, my recommendation is to go on the show and maintain your professionalism."

It would be useless to protest. The decision had been made for her, but she wasn't very pleased.

"I've got us popcorn, beer, chips, fried chicken and potato salad," Chere said, opening her apartment door to Jen.

Chere was determined to make it an occasion. She'd invited Jen over to her place to listen to the D'Dawg show. Even though *The Chronicle*'s public relations representative recommended it, Jen hadn't been looking forward to tuning in to the broadcast. She'd brought with her the bottle of wine she'd planned to share with Tre. Between the wine and Chere, listening might be made bearable. If nothing else Chere would provide running commentary and entertainment.

"This place is so you," Jen commented, entering.

Chere's apartment was flamboyant and outrageous just like the zaftig woman herself. A red sofa the size of a small monument took up most of the living room. Zebra toss cushions gave the impression you'd walked into a whorehouse. A large glass table was supported by brass elephant feet. The elephant had red painted toenails. Off to the side was a red-and-white tiled galley kitchen with red appliances.

"You want some of that fancy wine?" Chere asked when Jen was settled on the oversized couch.

"Sure."

Chere was dressed for comfort in an outlandish gold kimona and red vampy slippers with pouffed black feathers that swayed in the air-conditioning. She trotted off in the direction of the kitchen and stuck her head in the refrigerator. She removed a six-pack of some brand of beer Jen had never heard of, stacked a box that looked like it came from a fast-food chain on top of the beer, and opened a cupboard door. Chere retrieved a gigantic bag of chips, added it to the lot, grabbed Trestin's cabernet and hurried back.

"Time to eat," she said, arranging the goodies on the coffee table and plopping down next to Jen. "We got ten minutes before boyfriend comes on."

Jen politely sipped on her wine and thought about how to diplomatically tell Chere that all that cholesterol was slowly killing her, and then changed her mind. She nibbled on a chip, her stomach too queasy to ingest that much grease. Chere was already halfway through a meaty chicken breast.

"So you never did tell me what happened at that meeting," she said through a mouthful of food. "I had to hear from my girls that you agreed to go on the D'Dawg show. That came as a big surprise. Seems to me you sold out."

"I had no choice," Jen admitted. "I was ordered to."

"By who? Want me to sit on them for you?" Chere joked.

Jen watched Chere closely for a reaction when she said the name, "Ian Pendergrass."

"Why that dirty low-down… I'll squash him like the maggot he is."

Jen wasn't about to touch that one. "I'm sure he thought it was a good business decision," she said diplomatically.

By now Chere had worked her way through half the box of chicken. She was spooning large gobs of potato salad that came with the family-sized meal into her mouth. "Mmmm, this is good."

Jen wisely thought it best to concentrate on her wine and say nothing.

After a while Chere got up and toddled to a black lacquer-and-glass étagère. She flipped the switch on the stereo and fiddled with the knobs until she found WARP.

"This is D'Dawg coming to you live on WARP, the station that rocks."

"That man's voice would have me climbing out of my pants double time," Chere said, longingly.

Chere had finished the chicken and was swigging from a can of beer. Jen decided another glass of wine was definitely in order. She refilled her glass and took a big gulp. Trestin had superb taste in wine.

The air personality's voice sounded like liquid velvet. It was deep, sexy and hauntingly familiar. It drew you in. Jen knew if she'd met him she would have remembered.

"How come you don't know D'Dawg?" she said to Chere.

"Maybe I do and maybe I don't. Hard to keep track at times. The girls tell me he pretty much keeps to himself. He's not one for hanging at the clubs."

"I would think that's a good thing."

Beyoncé was belting out a soulful tune now. On purpose the DJ was dragging things out and the agony was excruciating.

"Our special guest tonight is Chet Rabinowitz," he finally announced between tunes. "For those of you who don't know, he's Mayor Rabinowitz's son. He's also the director of Flamingo Beach's Gay Alliance. Tonight he's going to tell us what he thinks about *Dear Jenna,* the latest addition to *The Chronicle.* Stay tuned. Things are bound to heat up."

Another round of tunes gave Jen time to top off her drink. Chere had started in on the chips and was noisily munching. Jen glanced at the clock. "That man is holding out until nine o'clock."

"What's so special about that hour?"

"You've got a captive audience. Kids for the most part are in bed. You're relaxing after dinner."

"What else do you know about this guy?" Jen asked.

"Only that he's single and fine," Chere answered through a mouthful of chips. "He pretty much stays to himself as I mentioned before."

"Where does he live?"

"Now, that I don't know." Chere who was half sprawled on the sofa flexed and arched her feet. The feathers on the silly-looking mules fluttered. "But you know there ain't nothing I can't find out. Why you so interested?"

Good question. Why was she? "Because it's nice to know what I'm up against."

D'Dawg took some calls before putting another tune on. Some had opinions about the upcoming election, others felt that Flamingo Beach's boardwalk and ancient arcade was well overdue for a face-lift. A few had questions about the upcoming interview but were urged to hold them until Chet Rabinowitz came on.

"Maybe we should make some popcorn," Chere suggested.

"Thanks, but I've had quite enough."

"You've hardly eaten," Chere said, noting that Jen still had a couple of chips she'd taken out of the bag clutched in one hand, and the chicken leg she'd deigned to part with on the plate in front of her.

"Now for the moment we've all been waiting for," D'Dawg announced. "In the house, and coming to you live from Flamingo Beach is Chet Rabinowitz, director of the Gay Alliance. He's a man you all know. Chet is a florist and part owner of All About Flowers. He's also our mayor's son. What do you have to say for yourself, my man?"

"I'm very pleased to be invited on the D'Dawg show. You're doing a fine job of keeping the folks of Flamingo Beach up on current events," a high-pitched and very nasal voice said.

Chere rolled her eyes and chortled. "That's a good one. Prying into citizens' business is now called current events."

"Shhh. Let's hear what else he has to say."

"Thank you. Let's hope the good citizens of Fla-mingo Beach are in agreement. I need ratings, y'all. Tell everyone you know to tune into the D'Dawg show. But you didn't come on the radio to talk about me. We're here to discuss people's reactions to last Sunday's column. There's been a lot of tongue-wagging and people wanting *Dear Jenna*'s head. You've been fielding calls from angry townspeople and answering e-mails. Care to comment?"

"Well, I think it was an unfortunate choice of words…"

"What words are we talking about? The advice to the parent or a particular word?"

What an instigator! The host sure knew how to stir things up.

"Well I don't know if I would have given the same advice," Chet said, "The son is still in the closet. Suggesting to his mother she find him the right woman is insulting. I might have recommended therapy. Clearly he has issues."

"You hear that, y'all?" D'Dawg chortled. "You know what I think is insulting, that slur that was used. Flip through a dictionary—that word means strange or odd. You're neither."

Jen held her breath, certain more rhetoric would be coming.

"And from here on," Chere said, heaving her bulk off the couch and stabbing a fingernail at Jen's nose. "It goes downhill. Every circuit's going be busy on the air and off."

Jen raised a finger shushing her. "Let's listen. No point in getting riled up."

But she was already riled up, although she was less vocal about it than Chere.

Chapter 7

"Is it the word *queer* that's got everyone so bent out of shape?" Chet asked, his voice taking on even more of a lilt.

"That's it. That's exactly the word!" D'Dawg shouted. "You said it. I didn't."

"Personally I didn't find it offensive...."

"You didn't?"

"Yes!" Jen said, pumping her arms in the air. "Yes, thank you. There is a God."

"There's a 'but' coming," Chere warned. "Just wait and see."

She must have ESP because right on cue it came.

"...but others did and that's what's important. The gay community's worked very hard to eliminate epithets from the layperson's vocabulary. Words like *queer, fairy, light in the loafers, fag,* that kind of thing. Those were all considered inappropriate words deemed insensitive and hurtful."

"And you've made great headway," D'Dawg said. "Your efforts have contributed to the almost total elimination of gay-bashing in this town. You've mainstreamed the word *gay.* Those with alternative lifestyles are now accorded respect. Look at how far we've come. In some states marriage between two people of the same gender is sanctioned and accepted. About time I say."

"We?" Jen said aloud. "No wonder this guy came after me with both barrels. The dog's gay."

She'd taken to calling him "the dog" because, like a salivating canine on a bone, he just wouldn't back off. Now she knew he'd taken her comments to heart and was making going after her his personal crusade.

"Nah, I don't think so." Chere's head moved from right to left. "My girls say the equipment works fine but it's been out of commission for the last few months, and no one knows why."

"He's probably found himself a partner."

"No, I would have heard."

Chet was now yakking a mile a minute. He was passionate on his subject. "Even more states need to get with the program," he said. "Homosexuality is a reality in today's world. There's at least one of us in each family. Progressive companies are offering insurance to those in same sex partnerships so…"

"Which makes it even more disheartening when a newcomer to our town sets our effort back several years."

"Our," Jen pointed out. "See." She and Chere exchanged looks.

"Nah," Chere repeated, "Don't even go there. I told you he was all male."

"You had to have been offended by Dear Jenna using the word *queer,* instead of gay," WARP's host stated, no longer interested in beating around the bush.

"As I said before," Chet answered, "I didn't take it personally. I wasn't offended. 'Queer' is perfectly acceptable lingo today."

"So why the huge uproar? Why are my phones ringing off the hook? Why are people looking to hang and quarter *Dear Jenna?*"

"It's her advice that was a problem." Chet was speaking rapidly now, warming to his subject. "There's nothing you can do to change genetics.

That's what *Dear Jenna*'s trying to get this mother to do. She's trying to force the man into becoming something he's not. That's just wrong."

"Hold that thought," D'Dawg practically shouted. "We've got to make time for our advertisers."

During the break, Chere helped herself to yet another beer while Jen settled for a chilled bottle of water. She needed all her wits about her to plan her counterattack when it was her turn to go on WARP.

The following fifteen minutes D'Dawg entertained questions and comments. It seemed all of Flamingo Beach had tuned in. The conversation now shifted from the perceived slur to the advice that was given. The audience was equally divided and some had quickly changed positions. Instead of wanting to crucify *Dear Jenna,* they were now praising her for staying on the cutting edge.

In many ways Jen considered this a victory. She had won over many people, and that translated, hopefully, to new fans and more newspapers purchased.

At the end of the hour, D'Dawg called a halt to the questions. He thanked Chet and confirmed that Chet's dad, Mayor Rabinowitz would be on the air the following night.

"It wouldn't be fair if Aunt Jemima doesn't have her say as well," D'Dawg said. "Two nights from now WARP's going to have Jenna on this show. Stay tuned—temperatures in Flamingo Beach are about to rise even more."

"What about me?" Chere said, pointing to her ample chest. "Don't I deserve my fifteen minutes of fame too? I help you."

"You'll have more than fifteen minutes," Jen said high-fiving her. "*The Flamingo Beach Chronicle*'s distribution's about to increase. That should mean money in both of our pockets. There's a cruise in our future. We'll be slurping down those Bahama Mamas in no time."

"From your mouth to God's ear."

Chere's palms were in the air, her overdeveloped bootie swung left, right, forward and center. She had that calypso music playing in her ear. In her mind she was already boogying on the upper deck of that cruise ship.

Temperatures had soared into the nineties, unseasonable for that time of year. Tre having awakened from his afternoon nap, decided lying poolside in the sweltering heat was a pleasant alternative to sitting around an air-conditioned apartment listening to tunes. He'd decided to bring his iPod with him.

He lay poolside on a cedar lounge chair with a

plump striped cushion under him, gulping iced tea, and pretending to be oblivious of the parade of hotties going by.

No more casual encounters, he vowed. They were a waste of time. At thirty-five, his focus needed to be on establishing a name for himself in the broadcast world. After that, the search would begin for an intelligent, attractive wife who wanted to have his children. She would have to be an independent woman, able to adapt to the crazy hours an on-air personality kept, and one who didn't easily get jealous.

His mother, for one, would be ecstatic. It would put an end to her efforts at matchmaking and they'd get along much better. Marva Jones-Monroe had taken to nagging him about his single status during her weekly phone call. Much as he loved his mother, she was getting on his last nerve.

Tre had hoped the high temperatures and clear blue skies would drive his intriguing neighbor, 5C out. He'd hoped she'd bring that bottle of red wine with her. Could be she was already lying poolside. Tre glanced at the sun worshipers. Most who occupied the loungers were reading books while sucking down beers and colorful concoctions. No Jen in sight so far.

Every now and then, a resident would jump off the

diving board or plunge into the pool headfirst. A few sat on the sidelines dipping a big toe into the water. The bar meanwhile did a brisk business. And the outfits were wildly tropical running from ultra-tasteful to the outrageously bizarre.

Tre tried not to analyze what these feelings of disappointment at not seeing Jen meant. He'd had fantasies of seeing her athletic body in a string bikini. But he doubted she would be that daring. He'd pegged her as the tankini type, showing a hint of midriff, and a lot of leg. And he'd hoped that if they hooked up again he could convince her to give dinner with him a try. Lunch as far as he was concerned had been very successful.

His attention turned to the shallow end of the pool where kids were splashing. A boy's and girl's laughter reached him as they tossed a ball back and forth. Some tenant must have visitors since the complex was restricted to adults that were age thirty and over. Not that Tre had anything against kids, he wanted a couple himself. But with the kind of hours he kept, he could only take noise in small doses. Now he was glad he'd brought a headset with him.

After getting his iPod going, Tre shifted onto his chest, rested his head on his arms, and drifted off. Something ice-cold trailed along his spine. His eyes flew open and he flopped onto his side.

"What the hell!"

"Well, good afternoon to you, too," Jen said in a chirpy voice.

His dreams of a string bikini and a shared bottle of wine shattered, Tre's gaze roamed over the red one-piece halter cut high on the thigh. It was a classy outfit but not overly suggestive, just like the woman herself.

"Is it hot enough for you?" he asked.

"I love this weather. When you spend most of your life in the midwest, the heat feels wonderful."

"That's right, you're from Ohio. What made you move?" Jen seemed to roll the question around in her mind. "Hold on a sec." Tre sprang up and dragged over a lounge chair that had just become vacant. "Might as well get comfortable."

He picked up his glass, offering her a sip of iced tea. She accepted, sucking long and hard on the straw. Ah, those lips.

"Thanks. That was just what I needed." She handed the glass back.

Tre signaled to the pool attendant. "Two iced teas, please." After the man had hurried off to get his order his attention returned to her. "So you were saying?"

Jen stretched out those shapely legs that he just

couldn't seem to get enough of. Her toenails were painted an attractive shade of coral and matched the nails on her hands.

"What was the question again?"

"What brought you here from Ohio?"

Tre got the feeling she hadn't forgotten the question but was buying time, thinking about how to respond.

"I needed a change."

"Why a change?"

Jen pursed her lips. "I turned thirty-two and decided it was time to take charge of my life. A girl can get pretty comfortable in Ashton. Too comfortable. I'd just broken up with my boyfriend when this opportunity to move to Flamingo Beach came about. I jumped on it and here I am. Where are our iced teas anyway?"

That was that. Topic closed.

Tre offered her another sip of his drink. Jen sucked it down gratefully and handed the glass back. "What about you? What brought you here? Don't tell me you are one of the rare natives?"

"Hardly." He chuckled. "I was born and, for the most part, grew up in a tough section of Detroit. I wanted an easier life for myself and any family I might have. When I moved to Florida, living was a heck of a lot cheaper than trying to make ends meet in a big city. Now of course, real estate prices are sky-high. But if I hadn't moved when I did I wouldn't have all of this and I wouldn't own anything." Tre's gesture encompassed their building and the surrounding complex.

The attendant was back. He set down their drinks on the arms of their chairs. Tre quickly signed the bill.

"It's my turn to treat," Jen interjected trying to wrestle him for the bill.

"No. I have an account. An iced tea is hardly going to break me."

"You own your apartment?" She looked at him questioningly. He assumed it was because she most probably rented.

"Almost," he answered. "I'm in the midst of negotiating the deal. You got in at the right time and should be able to as well. Flamingo Place is going condo. The insiders' price is substantially lower than what the management's telling outsiders. It's something you should consider if you plan on staying in Florida."

Jen's eyebrows arched. It was hard to read her. "Hmmmm, there's always that possibility. I think I'm going to take a dip."

"I'll join you."

For the next half an hour they swam laps and frolicked in the water. Tre found Jen easy to be around. She attacked life with gusto. It was refreshing to find a woman who didn't mind getting her hair wet. Strands of smooth, straightened hair skimmed her shoulders and at times got caught in her mouth. Her face now had a sun-kissed glow to it that hadn't been there before. Plus she had that lovely body that made his mouth water.

They toweled off and reclaimed their spots. When they were settled Tre said, "I'm wondering if you'd reconsider and have dinner with me." She opened her mouth but before she could get a word out, he continued, "I'm thinking an early dinner, something on the water. We'll watch the sun set and I won't keep you out late. I have to go to work myself."

Jen's hazel eyes flickered over his face. "Okay, you're on. What time will you be by to pick me up?"

"Five-thirty?"

"That's good."

And before Tre did something stupid like try to kiss her, he rolled onto his chest.

Half an hour passed. But no matter how much he tried, Jen's image stayed in his head.

Jen reminded herself not to expect much. She still wasn't sure how she felt about Trestin, yet she'd agreed to go out with him. Anyway, this wasn't exactly a date, more like a get-acquainted session.

She still didn't know the man's last name but she planned on remedying that tonight. She'd try to at least get a business card out of him.

Now to find something that was flirty and fun to wear but didn't send the message, "I want to go to bed with you." Not that her next-door neighbor was the type of guy most women would toss out of their bedroom. But she'd made a promise to herself, no more sex until she found out what a man was really made of. She'd learned her lesson from Anderson.

Jen tapped an impatient foot, dismissing one outfit after another. Her closet for the most part was conservative and very Midwestern. She needed to go shopping and add some color and style to liven things up.

It was hot. What did she have that was cool and stylish? Tre had mentioned something about a waterfront restaurant. Hopefully that meant casual. Jen tossed a handful of clothing on the bed and was about to sort through them when her cell phone played the upbeat calypso she'd programmed in.

It might be Luis. He was singing a slightly different tune since last night's broadcast. Jen had been inundated with calls from *The Chronicle*'s staff. She'd even gotten one from Eileen. Overnight she'd turned into some kind of celebrity. Preoccupied, she didn't check to see the inbound number.

"Hi, this is Jen."

"You busy?"

"Yes, Chere, as a matter of fact I am. I'm getting dressed for dinner."

She offered too much information. A big mistake.

Chere snorted. "You going out to eat and you didn't invite me."

"I was invited out myself."

"By who?" Chere's questions often violated the boundaries of decency. Jen let the silence drag out. "All right, be like that, don't tell me who you're having dinner with. I'd tell you who I was sleeping with."

"It's not like that," Jen clarified. "This is a sit-down dinner at a restaurant with hopefully intelligent conversation."

Chere snorted again. "Then he must be from out of town."

As outrageous as Chere was at times, she did make you laugh. For some unknown reason Jen decided not to fill her in.

"I have to go," she said. "I'm running late. I'll tell you all about it tomorrow. We're working from home. Be sure to get here on time."

Yet another snort followed. "I'll know all about who you were out with long before then."

"I'm sure you will."

Jen hung up. That conversation had taken five minutes off the time she had left. She sorted through the clothing on the bed and dismissed them one by one. Hurrying back to the closet she rifled through the racks, found a black peasant-style skirt with an abundance of ruffles at the back, and paired it with an orange camisole.

Digging through her drawers she found a black-and-gold scarf that, if tied around her waist, would give the outfit a lift. Jen quickly put them on and accessorized with gold hoop earrings and a wooden bangle.

Black sandals with a low heel completed the look. Now what to do about her hair? Should she wear it up or down? Down, she decided even though it was beastly hot. Pulled off her face and secured with sparkly little clips it would give a youthful look. She finished up by adding a touch of makeup. And just in time.

The doorbell rang. Jen hurried off to answer it. She opened the door to a yellow rose thrust at her.

"You look lovely," Trestin said, his eyes feasting on her face and then roaming her body.

"Thank you."

She accepted the rose, placed it between her teeth and in a playful mood, pirouetted before him.

He applauded. "Ready?"

"I just need to get my purse."

Jen placed the single bloom in a bud vase before picking up the rattan bag with the jaunty artificial flower attached to the front. It went with the bohemian outfit perfectly.

"I'm ready," she said. "Where are we going?"

"The Catch All."

"Good choice."

Hand in hand they headed down the hallway and toward the elevators.

Ida Rosenstein got off the lift as they stepped on.

"You're moving up in the world," she shouted at Trestin. "I'd take class over youth any day."

"I agree," he said as the doors shut smoothly behind them.

Chapter 8

"Have you decided?" Tre asked, closing his menu and setting it down on the table beside him.

"There's so much to choose from. It's a toss-up between the butterfly shrimp and the halibut," Jen said.

"Well I know what I'm having. That king crab has my name written all over it and I just might have crab cakes as an appetizer."

"Sounds to me like by the time you're done you might be all crabbed out." He noticed her grimace at her feeble attempt to joke. "I'm going to go for the shrimp and I'm going to have oysters on the half shell for an appetizer."

"Good for you."

Jen's menu joined his on the table. As if by some unspoken agreement they gazed out on the water where boats were moored, and a cocktail crowd stood on the outer deck enjoying the beautiful sunset.

The bars at The Catch All did a brisk business this evening dispensing drinks to a crowd there for happy hour. Both bars gave the illusion you were right at water's edge and so for that reason were immensely popular. Later some of the patrons would move over to the restaurant for a sit-down dinner.

Their waitress came, took their meal orders and left. Tre had passed on alcohol because he needed a clear head to interview the mayor later that evening. Jen had chosen not to have the wine he kept pushing on her. Tre had been trying to persuade her to sample a Zinfandel he'd recently been introduced to.

Bottled water was something they could agree on and did. Now each sat sipping from their respective glasses as the sun sank lower and lower, streaking the sky with a to-die-for pink and purple hue.

"Do you listen to the D'Dawg show?" Jen asked out of the blue.

Tre started. The question had come from nowhere and he was now fully alert.

"Can't say that I do. Why?"

That at least was the truth.

"Because I'd be curious to hear what you think about this controversy over the advice that columnist gave to the mother."

Tre shrugged and decided to play dumb. When put on the defensive, let the other person talk. "Fill me in," he said.

Jen succinctly told him what the problem was. She seemed a bit outraged that a fast-talking disk jockey wouldn't have kept up with modern day verbiage.

"Maybe the DJ did know but chose to yank the columnist's chain."

"And what purpose would that serve?" Jen argued, sounding more than a little irritable.

"Most disk jockeys like to stir the pot. You know, get people talking. The residents of Flamingo Beach aren't an easy audience. Sixty percent are retirees born in an entirely different era. Another fairly large percent are an influx from Cuba and Haiti, here in search of a better life. The rest are transplants in from a number of places in the United States, and attracted to beach-type communities because they can find a job in hospitality or elder care."

"If this guy just wants to stir the pot it's wasted energy. His time would be better spent taking a stand for a worthy cause."

"But didn't you say he took a stand? He stood up for gay rights."

"Because it suited his purpose," Jen lobbed back. "He took a commonly used word and twisted it for his own benefit just so he could up ratings on his awful program."

Tre gulped his water. He was getting a bit hot under the collar and he could only go so far in terms of defending himself. If Jen only knew who she was talking to....

"Hey," he said. "This really doesn't concern you and me."

"True."

Now it was Jen's turn to sip on her water.

"I never did get your last name," she said.

"I thought I told you," Tre bluffed.

"In that case I missed it."

"Monroe," he said and held his breath.

Please don't let her make the association between me and D'Dawg or I'm a dead dog. She's already made it clear how she feels about him.

"Trestin Monroe has a nice ring to it," Jen said. "Very old world."

He exhaled loudly.

The food arrived and they ate, even sharing a dessert afterward. With the exception of their little disagreement earlier on they were getting along quite well and Tre found that he liked her more and more. Jen had a wit that kept him on his toes and an interesting perspective on everyday life.

They were halfway through their shared dessert when a woman who'd been seated at the table to their right with a bunch of friends approached.

"Excuse me, but my girlfriends and I have a bet you're…"

"Sorry, this isn't a good time. I'm on a date."

She slunk back to her table looking crestfallen.

"Why were you so rude?" Jen asked. "You should be flattered. She's mistaken you for the supermodel Ty Beckham. What a body that guy has."

Tre wished she would notice his. He spent an hour at the gym every other day working on keeping fit.

"I didn't mean to be short—maybe I'll go over and apologize. Maybe I'll even buy the ladies a drink."

"Good idea."

Tre liked it that she didn't seem to mind when he left her, and headed over to the table where the women sat huddled, whispering.

He confirmed they were right as to his DJ status,

collected a business card from one of them and begged for their understanding, explaining that this was a first date and he hadn't told the lady about his career yet.

And then to sweeten them up a little bit he had the waiter send over another of what each of them was drinking.

"That was nice of you," Jen said when he returned. "Most people would have just left well enough alone."

"I'm not most people."

Jen looked at him for a moment, then a slow smile emerged. He found himself on pins and needles waiting for her response. Why did what she thought of him matter?

"Yes, I am beginning to realize you just might be special," Jen said.

And in just those few seconds all again was right with Tre's world.

An hour later, much later than he'd planned on being out, Tre dropped Jen off in front of their building. He'd wanted to kiss her goodbye but decided he'd save it for their next date, when he wasn't so rushed or concerned about getting to the radio station on time. His head needed to be in the right place when he interviewed Mayor Rabinowitz.

And there would be a next date. You could count on that. He'd enjoyed Jen's company immensely.

Tre drove to the radio station humming a tune and ignoring the little voice in his head that said, "proceed cautiously." At a gut level he knew he was playing with fire. He was in the process of negotiating the purchase of a home next door to a woman who sparked his interest. If things didn't work out, or if they were on different wavelengths, it could prove to be a most unpleasant living arrangement.

Tre was seated in his studio ten minutes before the show was scheduled to begin. Adrenaline surging, he shuffled through his notes. This was promising to be one heck of a broadcast. He'd scored a major coup getting Chet Rabinowitz, the Executive Director of the Gay Alliance on his show, plus his father, the mayor, and the advice columnist responsible for the controversy, and all on sequential nights.

The plan was to have the mayor who'd had several engagements that day, call in to be interviewed and then remain available to take questions from listeners.

The assistant producer, Bill, from the local community college stuck his head in through the open door. "Boris wants to speak with you," he said.

"Now? I'm on the air in a few minutes."

Bill waved a cell phone at him. "Now."

Tre accepted the phone that Bill pressed into his hand.

"I have exactly five minutes, Boris," Tre said.

"I know that. I just wanted to wish you luck."

Since when? Boris had never called wishing him anything before a show.

"Go easy on the mayor," he admonished. "This is a small town, deeply mired in tradition. There's a good possibility Solomon could be elected to a second term."

"Not to worry. I'll take that under consideration."

"Good. Now on with the show!"

More than anything Tre hated being indirectly asked to censor himself. He liked radio because it was free-flowing and easy, and he liked being able to ad lib as he went along. A good part of his popularity stemmed from his quick comebacks and witty one-liners. Well, he would just have to see how things went tonight. If Solomon droned on or got on his soapbox, D'Dawg would just have to liven things up.

"You're on the air in two," Bill said, two fingers raised in the air. He reclaimed the cell phone with his free hand.

Tre clamped on his headset and sat back. He nodded at the disk jockey who'd been on before him. The man gave him the thumbs-up sign and headed out.

"Um! Um! Um! It's D'Dawg coming to you live from the coast," Tre sang. "Yo, Flamingo Beach, you awake? This is the broadcast you all been waiting for. Last night it was Chet Rabinowitz, owner of All About Flowers and Executive Director of the Gay Alliance, saying his piece. Tonight Chet's old man, the mayor's, going to tell you what he thinks about this 'queer business.' And tomorrow, *Dear Jenna*'s coming on the air, y'all. She'll be stirring things up as only she can do."

Tre broke to play CDs. The music kept the audience entertained when he needed to take a break. At this hour of the night it was usually just him and the cleaning people, but tonight for some strange reason WARP's brass had been popping in under one pretense or another.

Boris had allegedly forgotten important paperwork. *He,* who never showed up unless he had to, was supposedly working late. Even the program director stuck his head into the studio to ask what Tre was doing after the show and if he wanted to go out for a beer.

Tre wasn't stupid. He knew he had to deliver. These broadcasts could make or break him. Even more than WARP's management, he needed the listeners on his side. They might not all agree with him, but his challenge was to keep them hooked and listening. The more people tuned in to WARP the better his ratings.

"Mayor Rabinowitz is on the line," Bill, the intern producer said, his finger pointing to a spot on the lit console. "He's got a tight schedule. He has to be off at ten on the dot. He's catching the redeye to Los Angeles."

"Gotcha."

Tre went back on the air and made the obligatory introduction. The mayor was actually not one of his favorite people but he would never voice that publicly. Solomon Rabinowitz was the type of old school politician who spouted a lot of hot air: promises, promises and little delivery. But he was well connected and in many ways Flamingo Beach was a "good-ole-boy" town.

Instinctively, Tre knew his glib homeboy style would not go over well with the seventy-two-year-old politician. Tonight he would have to tone it down a bit.

"Mr. Mayor," he began, "I know you're a busy man. Thank you for making the time to speak to your constituents."

"The pleasure is indeed mine. The good folks of Flamingo Beach are the ones who elected me. I am your public servant, here to do what I can."

Tre wasn't sure what exactly that was. So far it had been *nada*. Roads badly needed repair and the educational system was abysmal.

Tre envisioned the mayor, a ruddy-complexioned man with a fringe of hair circling his sunburned pate. He was given to wearing pastel jackets, suspenders and bow ties. The man spent most of his day at the exclusive Flamingo Beach Yacht Club yakking it up with his buddies.

"Last evening, your son, Chet came on the air," Tre said assuming his D'Dawg persona. "He let it be known he's gay. How does his daddy feel about his choice?"

Tre held his breath, waiting. The comment and question had just slipped out. It was just his nature to push the envelope.

"Chet is an adult," the mayor said carefully. "I respect whatever choices he makes."

"So you're saying you support his alternative lifestyle."

"I am saying I support his choices."

"Isn't that the same thing?"

"No, it's not."

"Please clarify your statement."

Through the glass pane, Chet saw Boris's expression. His camel-colored skin had taken on a pinkish tinge. In the next glass-enclosed studio, he'd clamped on headphones and was listening to the broadcast. Clearly he was growing uncomfortable.

"We live in the United States, a country that embraces people of every race, nationality, creed and lifestyle. Give us your poor...blah, blah, blah," Mayor Rabinowitz preached. "...We encourage freedom of speech. The women's movement has made incredible headway giving women in many states the right to choose."

What a bunch of rhetoric the mayor was spouting. He was going around in circles, pandering to both sides of the fence. If he didn't cut through the bologna quickly he would lose his audience.

"Agreed, Mayor, but what I want to know is where you stand on the subject of gay rights?"

"What does my opinion have to do with tonight's discussion?" the mayor came back with. "I thought I was here to talk about the controversy that's consuming this little town of ours."

"Exactly," Tre shot back. "And that is why I and the good citizens of Flamingo Beach need to know where you stand on the issue of gay rights. What do you think of this *Dear Jenna* using a controversial word like *queer?*"

Boris in the adjoining Studio removed his headphones. He appeared to be in the midst of a coughing fit.

"I believe," the mayor said emphatically, "that this whole controversy has gotten out of hand. I believe *Dear Jenna* was doing her job and meant no harm. Her words were taken out of context by people who may not have kept up with the current jargon."

"Hold that thought while we break for our advertisers, the people who help pay WARP's bills and my salary!" Tre shouted. "When I get back I'll be opening the lines for questions."

Tre tossed off his headphones and went off to speak with Boris who was gesturing frantically.

Chapter 9

"Yeah," Jen crooned, dancing a little jig. "I've got the mayor on my side, that's got to count for something."

Tonight she'd accepted Eileen Brown, the advertising manager's invitation to come over to her place. Jen had agreed because it was time she got to know more people, especially people she had something in common with. As entertaining as Chere was, the two came from different social backgrounds, and had unrelated goals.

"Yes, it helps to have Solomon on your side,"

Eileen answered. "He is old-school and well-connected. And he still carries some clout in this town."

"I was under the impression he was facing stiff opposition in the upcoming election."

"True. Miriam Young is a fairly recent transplant. She moved up from Miami about four or five years ago. She's a single parent, in her forties, who has made a point of staying in touch with the people. She recognizes the problems and shortcomings of a small town and she's youthful enough, optimistic enough, and energetic enough to want to fix them. She's not above canvassing door to door and in fact already has."

"It sounds like she stands behind what she's been saying. She's about the people and for the people."

"Exactly, while Solomon is out for himself."

"You must know him well."

"I do." Eileen's fingers smoothed the crevices on both sides of her mouth. She'd told Jen she'd returned to Flamingo Beach after a bout abroad to marry her high school sweetheart. She was also in her late forties.

"When you're born and raised in this town," Eileen continued, "you know pretty much everything there is to know about everyone. I left briefly to go away to college, and then I lived in Paris for a while, but nothing really changes in these small towns. The players stay the same…"

Jen held up a hand silencing her. "He's back on the air. That mouthy DJ's now taking questions. Do you know him? Is he always this way? Cocky, pushy and pursuing his own agenda?"

"Actually he's a pretty nice guy."

"Shhh, here comes the first question."

The woman who called in wanted to know if things were so boring in the town, that a comment made by an advice columnist could keep folks glued to their radios.

This voice of reason was hustled off the air and the next call taken. The man who clearly had an axe to grind was given more time. He was gruff and uneducated and took the conversation in a totally different direction. When he began quoting scriptures out of context, supporting his homophobic position, Jen rolled her eyes.

It was the third caller who got to her. She professed to be a friend of Ms. Mabel's and was calling in on the mother's behalf.

"Ms. Mabel's a friend of mine," she said. "She thought *Dear Jenna* gave great advice. She's put an ad on Café Singles. You won't believe the responses she's gotten. Let it be known Ms. Mabel has no issue with the columnist. So you people shouldn't."

"Yes!" Jen yelled again. "Yes!" This time the jig evolved to a full-fledged dance.

The tables had turned and about time. Now that the mother had indicated publicly she was on Jen's side that should make the difference.

But the next caller had apparently not been listening or just didn't get it. He immediately began to lambaste *Dear Jenna* for what he called, getting the mother to "pimp" her son. Jen was just about over it. Emotions were already running high and there was no point in getting upset. It was what it was.

"Do you mind?" she asked Eileen, motioning to the radio and signaling she wanted to turn it off. "This was supposed to be a get-acquainted visit. I'd hoped to make Flamingo Beach my home for a long time to come. Are the townspeople always this volatile?"

"It depends. You have several that are old school or just not very well educated."

"You know what's ironic about this situation. My brother is gay. He lives in France. I've always respected his choice and I love his partner like a second brother."

Jen sneezed and reached for a tissue in her purse.

"What is it you'd like to know about the players in our wonderful town?" Eileen asked, while sipping on a glass of wine. She looked at Jen with some concern. "You're not coming down with a cold, are you?"

"Hopefully not." For the next hour, between sips of wine and mouthfuls of crackers and cheese, Jen quizzed Eileen about the irreverent DJ whose show she was to be a guest on tomorrow. She'd decided to take a page out of Solomon Rabinowitz's book and was taking advantage of remote access. She would go into work and from there call into WARP. Luis had indicated he would be there for support but regardless, she wasn't looking forward to this interview. Her intuition told her "the Dog" would go for the jugular. He would make it his mission to shake her up.

She could not and would not let that happen.

Tre had been expecting to hear from Jen and within twenty-four hours at that. If he was a betting man he would have lost. The evening went with no word and so had the better part of today. He'd thought that basic decency would have kicked in and she would have contacted him to at least say she'd had a nice time and thank him for dinner.

When five o'clock rolled around with still no call, he decided a quick visit next door to see if she was okay was more than justified. To Tre's surprise no one answered. Jen kept hours that were even funkier than his. Her occupation remained a mystery. More upset than he was willing to acknowledge, Tre retraced his steps and slunk back to his apartment to get some shut-eye.

His concentration now needed to be on the up-coming broadcast and rattling *Dear Jenna*. For the past two weeks the folks of Flamingo Beach had been all riled up. These last three days he'd kept them interested and tuned into the station. He needed to keep them that way.

This third and final interview could not be anticli-mactic. The audience, now better educated on the topic was already divided. Recently, the columnist's sympathetic and well-thought-out advice to a pregnant teenager who'd wanted to end her life, had gained her new fans. His career was now on the line; the manner in which he handled this third and final interview was critical.

With that in mind he went to bed to awaken an hour later feeling invigorated and with a new plan in mind. An hour and a half later he was at the station getting ready for the D'Dawg show.

Even though her cold had broken and she had a hoarse voice, Jen called in to WARP at the appointed hour. She was placed on Hold by the person screen-ing the radio station's calls. Despite Luis's being there, allegedly for support, his presence only made

Jen's stomach feel queasier and more nervous than it already was. She thought about all the angles the irreverent DJ could take. Since her using the word "queer" seemed to no longer be at issue, D'Dawg could attack her based on the advice itself and say she was meddling.

She would stand firm. Internet dating offered options. How otherwise were two busy people with similar interests going to connect? D'Dawg could say that she had no business encouraging a mother to be this involved in her son's life and that might very well be true. But what was different from two parents putting their heads together, and determining their son and their daughter were the perfect match, then setting them up? It was done all the time.

"You're on the air in five minutes, *Dear Jenna*," a production assistant said.

That gave Jen a few minutes to take a deep breath, compose herself and suck on a lozenge.

Luis who was seated next to Jen gave her the thumbs-up sign.

"Breathe and do a lot of listening. Don't let him rattle you. Take your time answering. When in doubt say, 'Well, let me think about that for a moment.'"

"You're on the air."

Jen's heart fluttered in her chest as the disk

jockey's deep, melodious voice came over loud and clear and he smoothly made the introductions.

"Coming to you live from WARP, the station that brings you those memorable tunes, is our third and final interview. It's the person we've all been waiting to meet. The woman whose name is on everyone's tongue. It's Flamingo Beach's own *Dear Jenna*. What's up, Jenna?"

"It's an honor to be invited on the D'Dawg show. I've enjoyed the past two night's broadcasts immensely."

"You hear that, people? *Dear Jenna* liked what I had to say."

Jen still wasn't sure what angle he'd be taking.

"So you straightened us out on the use of the word *queer*. We're all more educated now from having read your column."

Luis who was listening to the broadcast through a headset darted a look, frowning. There would be more forthcoming, Jen was sure. She waited, not acknowledging the host's words.

"I owe you an apology. My mama didn't raise no slowpoke. Apparently I need to keep up with current terminology. I'm going to eat humble pie and issue a public apology. I'm so sorry, Dear."

It didn't sound as if he was at all sorry. The *dear*

dripped with sarcasm and machismo. But what was she to say? This was a public airing. "Apology accepted," Jen said, graciously.

"What I still don't understand is why a grown man has to have his mama take care of his business for him," D'Dawg needled.

"That may very well be a question for the man's mama," Jen shot back, giving as good as she got.

D'Dawg guffawed. He seemed to be enjoying the exchange immensely.

"Maybe we should have Mama on the show," he said. "How many of you out there want to hear from Ms. Mabel? Someone called last night saying she was a friend. Maybe we need to have her hook us up with Mabel."

"And what purpose would that serve?"

"For one, we'd find out if your advice really works. We'll hear how many applicants actually applied for the girlfriend job. And we'd hear how Mama's going about screening out the ones she don't want."

"And you'd be violating the man's privacy. Both mother and son wanted to remain anonymous or Ms. Mabel would have chosen a very different medium to air her angst."

"Listen to these big words you're using. You sure you one of us?"

A direct shot. A put-down.

Luis's green-eyed gaze flickered over Jen. "Don't let him goad you."

But she was on a roll. She could be as combative as he if she chose. "As sure as I am a Dear," Jen said sweetly. "And as sure as you are that you're absolutely, positively straight."

Both of Luis's palms clapped the sides of his head.

D'Dawg chose that moment to announce they were breaking for commercials. Jen took a quick sip of water. She conceded that the DJ was very good at what he did. He'd left the listeners hanging. Phones were probably ringing all over Flamingo Beach.

"You're holding your own," Luis said. "Handling yourself well. Round two coming up."

It was a backhanded compliment. Luis had said it as if he didn't expect Jen to be that composed.

They were on the air again. Questions were coming fast and furiously now. Most of the population seemed to have forgotten what had started the controversy and the comments ran the spectrum, ranging from Internet dating to the Mama Boy's sexuality.

Right before Jen's interview ended, the next caller brought down the house.

"Son," the woman said, "if I knew that my writing to the paper about you would have caused this much commotion I wouldn't have done it, but I'm at my wit's end, boy…"

"Mother?"

And then WARP went to commercial again.

Jen was laughing so hard her sides ached.

"That's got to be a joke," Luis said sagely. "It's just another ploy on the broadcasters' part to send ratings skyrocketing through the roof."

"If that's so, D'Dawg gets an A-plus for ingenuity. It doesn't get much funnier than this. He's got to be one confident man. I mean one portion of the audience is going to believe that was his mother calling, and another segment will believe that he's gay. I've rethought my position."

"What does that mean?"

"I think I'd like to meet him."

The funny thing was Jen meant it. The wisecracking, fast-talking disk jockey with the familiar-sounding voice fascinated her. She wanted to put a face to a name. She wanted to see the confident-sounding man in the flesh. In her mind's eye she pictured a dark-skinned man with a shaved head and an earring in one lobe. He'd be dressed in something hip and trendy. And he was used to women eating out of his hands.

There were several things she could learn from him. One was definitely the art of self-promotion.

And promotion was what it was about; making sure your name stood out.

D'Dawg was hip, fast-talking and glib. Maybe it was time for her to get with the program.

Jen might have left Ashton, Ohio, but there was still a lot of Ohio in the girl.

It was time to change that.

Chapter 10

Off the air, Tre let loose with a loud string of curse words.

"Mother…"

He listened distractedly as Boris and the other shirts who'd hung around congratulated him on a fabulous show.

"What a great idea," one of them said, "Having someone call up and pretend to be that boy's mother."

If they only knew.

"Ingenious," Boris said, swept along by their enthusiasm. "That interview ended on the perfect note."

"Thanks. I'm leaving. I need to get something to eat," Tre said, mindful of his rumbling stomach and knowing he had a phone call to make that didn't require witnesses.

"Can we buy you dinner?" one of the executives asked. "You've more than earned it."

Tre graciously declined. He endured more back-slapping, high-fiving and exuberant compliments before slipping away.

Seated in his car he decided takeout might not be a bad way to go. He was in no mood to deal with a noisy restaurant or running into groupies looking for something more than an autograph. He wanted cool air-conditioning, relative solitude and time to calm down. Marva had just pushed his last hot button and he was sick to death of her embarrassing him. It was she who'd called. He knew his own mother's voice and at times still heard it in his sleep.

Whatever had possessed her to do something so stupid as to write to an advice columnist? Not any old advice columnist, mind you, but one that lived in his town. He knew she'd been getting antsy about his single status, but to imply that he might be playing for the other team. Well that was outrageous.

Tre had always been an open and fair-minded individual. He respected other's choices even if they weren't his. But his mother of all people should know he was one-hundred-percent male. He'd brought home at least two women to meet her although that was a long time ago.

Using his cell phone, Tre ordered fried chicken, macaroni and collard greens, favorites of his since childhood. Tonight would be about indulging. Tomorrow about weights. That last call had come out of left field and now in a surprising turn of events he was the one on the defensive and *Dear Jenna* had turned into the flavor of the month.

The most important thing that had happened was this third and final interview had been a big hit. He was on his way to the big times.

After picking up his food, Tre decided to hurry on home. As he entered his apartment he noticed the flashing light of his answering machine. He groaned. It was after midnight and he was just too tired to fend off fans or entertain questions. But late hour or not, his mother needed to be dealt with.

He dished food onto his plate, and grabbed a bottle of beer from the refrigerator. He rarely indulged in alcohol after his show but tonight he'd earned it. Then he returned to the living room, placed the plate on his lap, and sat back on the sofa. Cell phone out, he pressed one little button with the programmed number.

As he waited he thought about how times had changed. When he was growing up, no one ever called anyone in Detroit after nine or it was considered rude. But this was his mother, Marva, and after the stunt she'd pulled earlier, she should be expecting his call.

The phone rang a considerable number of times. Tre knew she was home. It was a weeknight and her bingo game ended at ten. He disconnected and punched in the number again.

This time he got a croaky, "Tre is that you?"

"Yes, Mother."

"You never call me on a weeknight." She sounded groggy, half-asleep. "Is something wrong, baby?"

"What do you think?"

"Oh, you're mad at me. I know that voice."

Mad was an understatement. He took a bite of chicken and figured he'd let her stew.

"Furious," he said after he'd chewed. "What did you think you were doing calling me on the job?"

Marva Jones-Monroe sighed heavily. "It's the only time I can reach you, baby. You no longer have time for me."

"You called me on the air, Mother! And that's just not true. We talk every Sunday after you get back from church."

Marva's tone reached a crescendo. She was fully awake now. "I was on the air? Everyone heard me?"

"Yes, they did, Mother, loud and clear. And now I have to worry about people thinking I'm gay. You need to stay out of my business. I can find my own bride without your help."

Another labored sigh followed. "I wish you would. It doesn't hurt to look at the letters and photos I have. These women are seriously marriage-minded. Make your old mother happy, give me grandkids before I die."

Tre took another huge bite of chicken and spooned macaroni into his mouth. His mother, much as he loved her, at times frustrated him.

"I'm not interested in meeting any of your choices, Mother," he said. "You're in no danger of dying any time soon. You're only in your late fifties. Our family lives long into their nineties. That gives you another forty years of productive living ahead. Plenty of time to play with grandchildren."

This time his mother's voice sounded muffled and as if she was close to tears. "That's not what the doctor says. I didn't want to tell you this before but I'm not well."

He felt the familiar tightening in his chest. His mother was the only one he had left in the world. His brother was a waste, just as their father was. His father had stuck around long enough for Marva to get pregnant and then he'd run off with someone else. Who could blame Tre for being gun-shy about marriage? He refused to be like his father. When *he* married it would be forever and ever.

"What's wrong this time, Mother?" Tre asked in a gentler tone.

"The doctor says my blood pressure is up and my sugar's high."

Tre bit his tongue. What he really wanted to tell her was that she needed to go easy on the sweets, and that would take care of at least one of her problems. And even though he didn't know whether to believe her or not because her grumblings of illness had become a familiar ploy, he needed to pay attention.

"What did the doctor say? What measures are you taking to get these issues under control?" he probed.

"I'm taking my medication if that's what you're asking," his mother said defensively.

"Are you exercising?"

"I walk when I can. But Mrs. Calhoun isn't around as much as she used to be since she took up with that man."

As he thought, poor eating habits and lack of

exercise were probably contributing to his mother's problems.

"Dr. Habib thinks I need a vacation, a break away from all this pressure," Marva whined.

"What pressure, Mom?"

"There's pressure and stress just in daily living."

His mother was retired and living comfortably on her pension and the monthly allowance he sent her.

"So where are you thinking of taking this little vacation?" Tre asked.

"Someplace warm and relaxing."

Uh-uh! Here it came. Sometimes it was best to play dumb. He got up, taking his plate with him and entered the kitchen and set down the dish on the counter. "Hawaii would be a good choice. You've said for quite some time you'd like to go there."

"True, but I was thinking more like Florida. I haven't seen my son in some time. I miss him."

Even though he knew he was being manipulated, put like that, what could he say?

"Uh, Mother, have you removed that ad from the Internet yet?" he asked, changing tactics.

"Of course not, silly. I've had so many nice women respond, one of them has to be your Ms. Right."

God, she was trying his patience.

"I'll tell you what, Mother," Tre finally said. "As

soon as you cancel the account I'll send you a ticket to come down to Florida."

"You will!" Marva screamed so loudly she almost pierced his eardrum. "You're bringing me to Florida? I'll get to see Flamingo Beach?"

"Yes, Mother."

"And I'll be there a minimum of two weeks?"

"Yes, Mother."

Two weeks of his mom might just drive him to drink, but at least she would be under his watchful eye until the hubbub died down.

"Send the ticket tomorrow." An unmistakably loud yawn filled his ear. "I need to go to bed now, son. I'm not as young as I used to be." The phone was then promptly disconnected. Marva had gotten what she wanted from him.

Tre, fond as he was of his mother, was well aware of her shortcomings. Meddling was definitely one of them.

Marva meant well but he really wished she'd think before she acted. He'd have to figure out a way to make her embarrassing call to the station work for him. He could pass it off as a joke, designed to be attention getting and leave the listening audience speculating.

The more Tre thought about it the more he liked the idea. He could make his mother's call work to his advantage. He'd just have to put a spin on it. Maybe that would be the new hot topic he could pursue. "Meddling mamas and their sons." It made him chuckle. It was bound to be a sensitive subject and elicit a highly emotional response from the audience.

Deep in thought, he almost missed the envelope shoved under his door. He bent to retrieve it, and not recognizing the handwriting, frowned. Had the neighbors, actually one in particular, resorted to complaining about his music in this manner? He hated anonymous notes.

Envelope in hand he returned to the kitchen to have his second beer of the evening, reasoning he still wasn't loose. How much excitement could one man take?

Tre uncapped the bottle and used a knife to open the envelope's flap. He grinned. This was totally unexpected. It helped brighten what so far had been a fairly dismal day. Jen had written to thank him for a lovely evening.

It was the P.S. that got to him. She wanted to reciprocate and was inviting him to her apartment for dinner if he was free some night later that week. Of course he'd make a point of being free. He had a well earned day off coming up on the weekend.

It was too late to call or go knocking on Jen's

door. He planned on responding in the same fashion she had. He would write her a note, something he hadn't done to any woman in years.

Feeling like a little boy who'd been given his first Game Boy, Tre went in search of the expensive stationery one of his groupies had given him for Christmas.

He would slip his acceptance under Jen's door. And he would make sure dinner happened on a weekend when they both weren't rushed. There would be plenty of time to explore Jen St. George and find out her likes and dislikes.

Sleep was impossible now. His imagination had taken over. Tre turned to his trusty stereo and some of his favorite tunes to help him drift off. He was almost half-asleep when he heard a banging on his wall. Surely his music wasn't that loud? He could barely hear it. He tossed off the covers and using his elbow, banged back.

Regardless of whether he found Jen St. George intriguing or not, he wasn't about to let her bully him. Reaching over, he turned up the stereo a notch. Then he closed his eyes and drifted.

It had been the right thing to do, writing a handwritten thank-you and inviting Trestin to dinner. He'd helped her out when she was in a bind.

Jen had awakened early that morning, dressed quickly and rushed out the door only to discover the Miata's front tire was flat. She'd called AAA, the motor club she belonged to, but there would be at least an hour's wait before they came.

Jen had been frustrated and feeling helpless when along had come Trestin. He'd noticed her visible distress, and overriding her halfhearted protests had gotten the flat tire changed in a matter of minutes. Thanks to him she'd only been a few minutes late to work.

True, there was also an ulterior motive for inviting him to dinner. Jen had begun to suspect he might be employed by *The Southern Tribune*. After all, working in communications could mean just about anything.

Someone had mentioned the competition was actively interviewing, a psychologist dubbed *The Love Doctor*. The idea was to have this credentialed doctor compete with her *Dear Jenna* column. Trestin, if he did indeed work for *The Tribune,* might be able to confirm that. She needed to know what she was up against.

Jen still hadn't made up her mind about Trestin. He seemed to be a person of multiple personalities. He could be arrogant and overbearing at times, kind and intuitive at others. They'd had a wonderful dinner filled with interesting conversation. While she wasn't necessarily looking to get close to anyone in the same building, it was nice to know that in a pinch, like she'd been in a few days ago, he could be counted on. But she'd damn well make sure she didn't get too dependent on him.

Growing up in foster care with a brother who was different had taught her not to rely on anyone. In the blink of an eye, just when you were starting to feel secure, things changed, and you inherited a new set of parents. Anderson, her ex, had been a man she had trusted and look at how that turned out.

She wanted to see how Trestin handled himself on territory other than neutral ground such as the pool and restaurant. Would he be a gentleman? Dinner would be the test.

Now she waited for him to get back to her.

It was too early for bed. Maybe she would turn on her computer and Google this "Love Doctor." She'd just booted up the computer when the phone rang.

"You in bed?" a raucous female voice inquired.

"No, Chere, I'm not."

"Just wanted to report the whole town's buzzing about how you handled D'Dawg. 'Course I didn't let on you and me work together."

Of course she didn't.

Chere continued in her usual overly effusive manner, giving her opinion that the call from D'Dawg's mother had been staged. Jen was of the same mind as she. It seemed too much of a coincidence. The outrageous scene had to have been cooked up by the ambitious host to pump up his ratings.

"What do you know about this psychologist *The Southern Tribune*'s supposedly hired?" Jen asked Chere.

"You mean The *Luv* Doc?"

"Doctor Love."

"I heard they been interviewing a bunch of dorks. They would have gotten me cheaper. Betcha I can teach the peoples a thing or two."

"I bet you could. Listen, I have to go."

"Wait!" Chere shouted. "You still never told me who you had dinner with. Betcha I know."

Pretending not to hear, Jen hung up on her.

Jen's concentration was off as she brought up a list of possible *Doctor Loves*. The possibilities were endless. One "love doctor" in California wrote a column for a popular e-zine. Another author out of Chicago was a constant guest on *The Dr. Phil Show*. He helped the popular television personality dispense advice. There was even a porn queen with the name. Her outlandish attire reminded Jen of Chere.

Jen ruled out the porn queen as a viable candidate. *The Southern Chronicle* wouldn't stoop that low now, or would they? Jen's thoughts shifted to her next-door neighbor. He could be charming, arrogant and inconsiderate. But there was still something about him that was exciting and appealing. He was the kind of guy with a youthful outlook who would never grow old at heart, but whom you could grow old with. She wasn't looking, but if she was, she would opt for— stable and safe. Trestin Monroe was neither stable or safe.

A *thump, thump, thumping* came from next door. Her next door neighbor was back at it. Jen tried her best to shut out the noise but her skull felt as if a nail had been driven through it. Enough already. She pounded a fist against their shared wall.

"Keep it down, please!"

In reply, the music swelled even louder. The only way to get her point across was to give Trestin a taste of his own medicine. She turned on her surround sound and sat back to wait.

In about ten minutes there was a banging on her door. Jen smiled triumphantly. One point for her. Let the man experience what she did the minute she closed her eyes. She'd ignore him and pretend not to hear the rapping.

The banging continued, louder this time.

"Security, Ms. St. George!" a gruff voice shouted. "We'll need you to turn off your music."

Security? Shit! As unresponsive as they'd been to her previous complaints about 5B, she hadn't expected this.

Jen turned off her stereo hoping that would be the end of it, and she wouldn't receive a nasty note from the management company.

Life was so grossly unfair. If anyone should be cited for disturbance it was that inconsiderate jerk she'd felt the need to invite to dinner because of one good deed.

Why, oh why, had she allowed him to bait her?

Chapter 11

"I thought I said seven," Jen mumbled as one hand of the clock slowly made its way to the half-hour position. "Could I have been wrong?"

Everything was ready. The chowder was in the pot just waiting to be served. The shrimp and scallops were simmering on the stove. She'd serve them in cream sauce with mushrooms over bow-tie noodles. The crisp sourdough rolls fresh from the oven had already been placed in a wicker basket and now sat on the kitchen counter.

In the middle of the dining room table she'd set

down a vase holding her favorite flowers. Sunflowers. Maybe it was the color but just one look at them and her mood shifted to optimistic.

When the phone rang, she frowned. "Please don't tell me he's canceling at this late date," Jen muttered out loud, simultaneously grabbing the receiver.

"Yes?"

"Watcha up to?"

Chere. The woman had uncanny ESP.

"I been thinking of taking myself to this new bar that just opened. You want to join me?"

"I'm afraid I can't. I'm busy."

Silence. A foreign sound for her administrative assistant. She must be between men. Jen had never known Chere to be available on a Saturday night.

"Busy doing what?" Chere asked through what Jen imagined to be chomping. "Chuck those letters for one night and come out on the town. Please!"

Jen sighed. She'd better nip this right now or Chere would arrive over, trying to convince her to come.

"I have dinner plans," Jen said firmly. "Maybe we can do a movie tomorrow."

"Who you have plans with?"

The woman had no shame. "That's for me to know and you to find out."

Chere cackled. As always she took the rebuke in good stride.

"Girl, leave it to me to find out. Nothing's sacred in this town."

"I'll check in with you tomorrow," Jen said and quickly hung up.

The doorbell rang, and about time too. Jen put an eye to the peephole and satisfied it was Trestin threw the door wide.

He stood on the threshold, for once looking uncertain.

"I'm sorry I'm late," he said. "My peace offering wasn't ready." He handed her a box tied with several colorful ribbons. "This is to make up for the other night. We have Camille Lewis to blame for that visit by security."

"Interesting lady." And to think she'd thought it was him calling security.

He rolled his eyes. "The understatement of the year. Rosa makes the best key lime pie in town. I ordered in advance but there were problems with the refrigeration. In any case I had to wait."

It was on the tip of Jen's tongue to tell him he could have called. But bringing the pie was a thoughtful gesture on his part, especially given they had no relationship. She'd expected him to show up swinging his two empty hands.

"And I have something else for you," he said handing her a square flat package that was carefully wrapped.

"Should I open it now or later?"

"Later. Maybe when you're alone."

Jen thanked him and stood aside so that he could enter. Trestin's gaze swept the room. "You have great taste. Are those antiques?"

"Yes, I know, very un-Florida in the land where pastels, chrome and glass prevail."

"Were they inherited?" he asked, his palm skimming the surface of the sideboard where she'd set out the dishes, cutlery and glasses.

"There was nothing to inherit. I grew up in foster homes."

He frowned. "Sorry."

She didn't want him feeling sorry for her. She was long over not ever knowing her parents.

"I was thinking we might have drinks on the balcony."

"I'll gladly play bartender," Trestin offered.

Jen pointed to the kitchen. "I have all the ingredients for margaritas. They're not a very masculine drink but the temperature outside calls for something cool and soothing."

"You have that right, the temperature I mean, not the masculinity thing. There are still real men who drink margaritas." He winked at her. "In fact I would love one."

She decided to leave it alone.

Trestin's cadence reminded her of someone, but right now she could barely think straight. His six-foot-two frame was too close to her, and his smooth dark skin made the white linen shirt look like it was exclusively made for him.

"There's always beer and vodka if you prefer," Jen offered, speaking quickly.

"I'm sticking with margaritas."

She left Trestin seated on the balcony, plopped in the pasta and hurriedly made up a batch of the quenching drink. Jen returned minutes later, carrying a pitcher and two glasses on a tray. She set the tray down and handed him one.

"You'll join me."

"But of course."

After pouring a glass she stood next to Trestin and stared out on the ocean. Dusk was giving way to night and the last hopeful rays of sunshine illuminated the gray-green water.

"You wouldn't by chance have tuned in to WARP

and heard Mayor Rabinowitz the other night?" Jen asked.

"Not sure why I would do that."

"Why wouldn't you?"

For someone claiming to be in communications, he seemed so uninformed and uninterested in the happenings in their tiny town. Jen remembered asking him a similar question about the D'Dawg show when they'd had dinner previously. His answer had been about the same. What could be occupying his time so totally that he wasn't keeping up with current events?

"Exactly what kind of communications are you in?" she asked.

Was it her imagination or was that a sickly tinge of gray shading his ebony skin?

"I'm a journalist of sorts."

He spoke carefully. Too carefully.

She was beginning to think that what she suspected was true. He worked for the competition. In that case he was a really good person to know. Then again maybe he was just yanking her chain.

"I brought up the *Dear Jenna* controversy before and you hadn't heard of it."

"What about it?"

"I'd think you'd have an opinion."

"I do."

"So what do you think?" Jen was treading on safe ground. She looked nothing like the stuffy, uptight photograph of Dear Jenna, in the corporate suit wearing her Condoleeza Rice pearls and disfiguring glasses. The photo had to be at least ten years old when she'd first started out in the business.

"About the columnist using the word *queer?* Or about how this town seized on it like a dog with a juicy bone?"

"It was more like that horrible on-air personality fanned the flames into a huge fire. No, I was actually tuned in to the broadcast when the mother supposedly came on. Do you think it was really her or someone he put up to it?"

"I wasn't listening."

"But you just said—"

"Can we change the subject? Something smells delicious. I hope you didn't go through a lot of trouble."

"Actually I like to cook."

"Something else new I've learned about you."

"Is that a hint? Are you hungry," Jen asked.

"Famished."

"Then let's go inside where it's air-conditioned and eat."

Jen led him indoors, drained the pasta and began moving the items that made up the meal onto the sideboard. She'd set her tiny table with coral-colored table mats. Her napkin rings shaped like dolphins held jade cloth napkins pleated like fans.

"Help yourself," she said, gesturing to the laden sideboard. "I figured this way we would have more space."

Trestin needed no further prompting. He helped himself to the chowder and rolls, took a seat at the table and dug in.

"Delicious," he announced.

"Thank you. It's a new recipe. It turned out well."

After spooning the last of the chowder into his mouth, he piled his plate high with pasta, scallops and shrimp. Jen poured them both another margarita.

"So tell me," she said. "Why do you think this *Dear Jenna* woman's gotten so popular?"

"Because gossip sells. Our townsfolk have a lot of time on their hands or they wouldn't find other people's troubles so intriguing."

"*Dear Jenna* isn't a gossip columnist," Jen said inwardly bristling. "She's an advice columnist."

Trestin's fork paused midway from plate to mouth. "What's the difference?

"One spreads rumors. The other provides a service helping people."

Trestin snorted. "Services like telling an adult

man's mother to hook him up with some woman desperately wanting to get married."

Jen smiled. "You have been following the controversy. I take it you have something against marriage?"

He finished chewing and set his fork down. "Actually I don't. But I think an adult should do his or her own choosing."

"I think marriage, even plans to marry, can ruin a pretty good relationship," Jen offered

Trestin looked at her curiously. "I'm surprised to hear you say that."

"It's just that people immediately start having these expectations of each other." Jen was thinking of herself and Anderson.

"Like what?"

"Like one's going to tame the other. Like one of them needs to be home at a specific time to start dinner and God forbid they're not. Like one now owns the other."

Jen began gathering the dishes.

"You sound bitter." Tre stood. "I'll help you," he offered.

In the kitchen as they were stacking dishes into the dishwasher he continued, "I take it you've tried marriage and it isn't for you."

"No, I never have. I was engaged and I'm not interested in repeating that experience. Once the ring was on the monster got released."

"Ouch."

Jen's eyebrow shot up. "You're interested in getting married?"

"To the right woman."

"You are a diplomat."

"Well, I've been around enough marriages to know that both parties better be in sync on important issues. Because once those hormones stop revving, you'd better be on the same page when it comes to finances, goals and even raising children."

"Sure you haven't been married?" Jen teased, trying to lighten things up a bit.

"I'm sure. But I lived through an unhappy marriage." Jen glanced at him. "My mother and my father's. When the responsibilities that came with having two kids got to my father, he left. I've seen it time and time again with friends. Two people are getting along just fine, even living together. But they never discuss the vital issues and when reality hits home in the form of crises, one or the other is out of there."

"Uh-huh. Now you see why I'm not a proponent of marriage.

Trestin set the last plate in the dishwasher and closed the door. "I say date if you have to, get to know the person well over a period of time, although that's no guarantee. But it does help if the person shares your values and ethics and believes in a committed relationship."

"I'm not sure there's a person like that existing out there."

"You are jaded."

She supposed she was. Anderson had snowed her with his talk about soul mates and long-lasting love. He'd talk a good talk about fidelity and walking away from temptation. When it came down to it, he hadn't been able to walk the walk.

"What about kids?" Trestin asked. "Don't you want them? Or are you advocating having children out of wedlock?"

"I'm not planning on having any at all. It's tough being a single parent." Jen took the individual bowls of crème brûlée out of the refrigerator. "Shall we have these inside or out?"

"Inside. I'm fascinated by this conversation."

"Follow me into the dining area," Jen said, starting out.

Trestin set down the dishcloth he was drying his hands on and followed.

"You'd have beautiful children," he said, smiling at her.

"Think so?"

She placed a spoon in her bowl and began eating.

"In fact I'd be open to giving it a whirl."

She'd just been propositioned, or was it her imagination? Better set him straight right now.

"There's not a prayer of you and I going to bed tonight if that's what you're angling for. I'm not that kind of woman. I want to know my man well before I take that leap. And a leap of faith it will be after what I went through."

"I was joking," Trestin said with a perfectly straight face. "Lighten up. You'd have quite a bit of baggage to stow if you and I were to progress to the status of lovers."

"Fat chance in hell."

He was back to his cocky, arrogant self.

"Are you with *The Southern Tribune?*" Jen asked, taking the conversation in a safer direction.

"The newspaper? No, I'm not."

She wasn't sure she believed him. He trailed his fingers along her forearm and she wished he would stop touching her. His touch brought out the sensual erotic side of her that she hid from the world. "What about this doctor they're supposedly hiring?"

"Why would a newspaper need a doctor?"

Exasperated, Jen sighed. "I guess I'll just never get a straight answer out of you."

The pads of his fingertips traced a path on her arm, making her shiver.

"What have I been evasive about?"

She threw her hands in the air. "Everything. I had to push you for a last name. I still don't know what you do."

"Hey, simmer down. You're getting all worked up over nothing." Trestin now held Jen by the shoulders. She looked into his liquid brown eyes and forgot how much he could infuriate her.

His kiss began as a fleeting touch to her lips. When it became more intense it hinted at an even greater intimacy. He didn't push it though, just held her tightly before gently releasing her.

"I'd like to introduce you to my mother," he said unexpectedly. "She'll be visiting me in a week or so."

"What! Why?"

"Why not? You live right next door. It would be nice to know you if she needed a cup of sugar."

"That would be fine then."

Jen was thinking it might be interesting to see what Trestin's mama was like. Maybe she could even fill her in on the missing pieces of his life and talk to her about the things Trestin glossed over.

"Good. I'll bring her by."

When Trestin thanked her and kissed her goodbye his kiss was much more exploratory than demanding. Jen pushed him firmly out of her front door.

Chapter 12

"**B**aby boy, you've been holding out on me," Marva Jones-Monroe said the moment she spotted Tre's silver Porsche. "I didn't know you were living this large. Radio must be paying extremely well."

Clearly awed, she circled his vehicle, stroking the recently waxed surface and leaving streaks in her wake. She appeared perfectly fine to him, far from the sickly person she'd pretended to be.

Marva sprang into the front seat of the automobile before he could help her in, leaving him to load her many bags in the trunk and forcing him to tie a rope to hold the trunk lid together. They were off.

The twenty-minute drive to Flamingo Place went by quickly with his mother chatting away a mile a minute, filling him in on her friend Mrs. Calhoun's issues with arthritis.

On Tre's way up to the apartment, loaded down like a pack mule, he ran into Ida Rosenstein.

"Tre," she said loudly. "They're getting older, but at least your taste is improving. This one isn't as skinny as the one in 5C. By the way, I like that girl." She peered nearsightedly at Marva. "This ones got hips and big bazookas." Ida made a motion to indicate Marva's generous bustline. "And she's also old enough to be your mother." Ida snorted.

"I am his mother," Marva said indignantly, thrusting out her chest. "What girl in 5C?"

"She called me a mother," Ida said, going red in the face.

"No, she didn't," Tre swiftly interrupted. "This is my mother, Ida. The woman who gave birth to me."

"Wheew!" Ida said, wiping her forehead with the balled-up handkerchief she was holding in her hand. "I think I need a smoke."

"What girl in 5C?" Marva repeated as Ida fumbled through her purse looking for her pack.

"You stop by my apartment sometime this week." She pointed a crooked finger at her door. "5A, remember that. I'll make us Rob Roys and I'll fill you in." Ida found a cigarette, lit it and exhaled a smoke ring.

"I'd think this would be a smoke-free environment?" Marva said loud enough that even hearing-impaired Ida had to have heard, not that she would care.

Tre, using a hand that was less encumbered, whisked her away. "See you, Ida."

Somehow he managed to extract the apartment key from his pocket and get the front door open. His mother swept through as he struggled with her bags, managing to get them inside and setting them down before kicking the door closed.

Marva was already trotting around, touching his things and exclaiming. "My son, the radio personality has certainly come a long way from Detroit." She was through the French doors and out on the patio in a New York minute. "I think I'm going to love it here," she announced. "Smell that ocean. It's just what the doctor prescribed."

Little by little, Tre moved Marva's things into the guest room. The housekeeping service retained through the building had done a decent job of picking up and packing away extraneous items. And they should, he paid them well enough. Twenty-five dollars an hour for work that didn't require brain power was, in his opinion, highway robbery.

But linens were on the bed as well as the pretty comforter a saleswoman had convinced him to buy when he mentioned he was having an out of town guest. And now the room looked homey and welcoming. Too welcoming. Giselle, his "Cleaning angel," as she called herself, had even left a small vase of zinnias on the bureau.

"Tre, honey, where are you?" Marva called.

"Be right out."

He made a stop in the kitchen, poured them both iced tea and took the glasses out.

Marva was already ensconced in one of his deck chairs with the plump burgundy cushions. Her feet rested on the table in front of her.

"Thank you. This is quite the life," she said when he handed her her glass before taking a seat next to her.

"Yes, I've enjoyed living here. I just don't know how long I'm going to stay."

Marva paused with the glass at her lips. "Didn't you tell me you were buying the place?"

"Yes, that's in the works. But radio is a transient business. You go where there is work and where there's opportunity."

"Most wives aren't going to like that," Marva said sagely.

"In case you forgot, I don't have one."

Marva hoisted herself from the chair. "That's easily remedied. One of my pieces of hand luggage is filled with e-mails and photos I've printed out. You can have your pick, boy. There's everything from doctors to divorcees living on their exes' alimony looking for love. In fact I think I'll get them."

"Please don't do that." Tre whooshed out a breath. He should never have bought her a computer and printer for her birthday. Never! "You just got here, Mother. We'll look at them another time, okay."

Like hell he would.

"No, we'll look at them now," Marva insisted, "when you're not running off some place and I have your full attention." She toddled off, her ample booty swinging.

Two weeks of having her live with him would just about kill him.

Jen was happy to see that the town of Flamingo Beach had finally turned its attention elsewhere. Instead of *Dear Jenna,* the talk was now of the upcoming election—Solomon Rabinowitz versus the newcomer Miriam Young; the Flip-Flop Momma as she was called by the opposition, and not because she flip-flopped on issues, but because she'd been seen at a casual beach function wearing her flip-flops and blending in with the crowd. Her platform had been built on being about people and for people.

WARP's disk jockey now focused his attention on the upcoming election. He was busy poking fun at both candidates. And Jen, who had enough work to keep three people busy, had actually managed to delegate some to Chere who, for the moment, had knuckled down.

Jen was in the large cubicle she shared with Chere when Eileen Brown walked in. Chere was making her morning rounds catching up on any news she'd missed.

"Hi," Jen said, tearing her glance away from the computer. "I've been meaning to call you."

Eileen hitched a hip onto the edge of Jen's desk. It was probably the only spot she could find that wasn't cluttered.

"So," she said. "*The Tribune* has finally made an official announcement they're hiring this Love Doctor."

"About time." The rumors had been running wild. "What's this doc supposed to do that I'm not?"

"Sound official and flash his credentials. The whole idea was to stick it to *The Chronicle*, one-upmanship so to speak. I guess they feel a doctor with credentials lends a certain credibility to their new advice column."

"As opposed to my bachelor's degree in social work and my common sense," Jen finished.

"I suppose."

"Who did they pick? Anyone we know?"

"Let's talk over lunch," Eileen said. "That's if you're free."

"I'd love to have lunch."

"Good. We'll get sandwiches or salads and sit at one of those tables with the umbrellas out back. We'll catch up on everything."

"Sounds like a plan."

Just then Chere came toddling in, stopping short when she spotted Eileen. The sudden movement almost sent her pitching forward. She wore absurdly high platform sandals in a most unsuitable gold foil, definitely not shoes for an office. She grunted in Eileen's direction before wedging herself behind her small desk.

"I'll see you for lunch then," Eileen said, an amused expression on her face as she left.

"I don't like that woman," Chere said, not even waiting for Eileen to get out of earshot.

"Why not?"

"Because she thinks she's better than all of us.

She wears those clothes that look like they come from the back of some white woman's closet. And she talks like them, too."

"Eileen is classy," Jen said, letting Chere come to whatever conclusion she chose. "It takes a tremendous amount of courage to remain at the top of your game when for years you are the only African-American department head at *The Chronicle,* and you are a woman."

Chere sucked her teeth and rolled her eyes simultaneously. "She had plenty of help." Jen shot Chere a quizzical look but said nothing. Needing no encouragement Chere continued, "That old fart, Ian Pendergrass has always had a thang for her. He's got the hots for pretty much any woman of color."

New information. Perhaps too much information. Chere had just about confirmed how she'd fallen into an administrative job she wasn't qualified to hold. Doubtful she knew how to type and even if she could those nails would be a hazard. Today they were painted an odious neon-green.

"I have to meet with Luis," Jen said, successfully putting an end to the direction the conversation was taking. "He's become quite the micromanager lately. Now he wants to discuss the column before it's released."

"Better you than me," Chere said, sniffing and turning her attention back to the pile of letters waiting to be filed and catalogued. "And by the way I know who you've been dumping me for and hanging out with lately."

Jen stopped dead in her tracks. "Who?" she shot over her shoulder.

"Your next-door neighbor, the noisy one. The fine-looking guy who owns the silver Porsche."

Jen decided it best to just keep walking.

Later that day, she met up with Eileen for a late lunch. On purpose they'd chosen a time when most of the newspaper's staff was back at their desks and it wasn't stiflingly hot.

"Do you think you'll stay?" Eileen asked while they were picking their way through unappetizing salads.

The question had come out of nowhere. There must be a rumor circulating.

"Why wouldn't I stay?"

"This is a sleepy small town with very little to do other than go to the beach, fortify yourself at restaurants and drink yourself silly. You're a young woman, you might want a little more action."

"I was recruited from a small town," Jen reminded her. "Ashton is hardly happening."

Eileen pretended interest in her salad, popping a

cherry tomato in her mouth. "I just thought after that brouhaha with WARP you might be over us and considering moving on."

"Hardly. Things have settled down and I've settled in. I'm beginning to enjoy the town and its people."

"Good. Now I have a rather indelicate question to ask. What about dating? Have you met anyone interesting?"

"I'm not dating anyone if that's what you're asking."

Eileen placed the plastic cover back on what remained of her salad. "There isn't very much to choose from here in terms of eligible males. And if you're in the market for a single, professional African-American male you might be out of luck."

"So what's a single woman to do?"

"Date interracially or depend on friends to hook you up with someone they know. Mind you, he might be from out of town and he might or might not be divorced."

Dating was not a top priority, and she'd been too involved with her next-door neighbor to pay attention to what the town had to offer in terms of African-American males.

Eileen tossed the container holding the salad in the garbage. "There's a function coming up, given by Friends of the new African-American Library. It's going to be on Pelican Island where the library is. Barry, my husband, has two extra tickets. You're welcome to them if you'd like."

It was unexpected and certainly thoughtful. Jen was curious to meet Eileen's other half. She kept in mind Chere's comments about Eileen and Ian. It might very well be sour grapes on the part of her assistant but the older she got the more nothing surprised her.

"Thank you," Jen said graciously. "What kind of function is it?" She was thinking it might be a way to meet people. Professional people.

"It's actually a play. The troupe's from out of town. They're putting on *The Jackie Robinson Story*. There's a reception following the show, an opportunity to meet and mingle."

"That's so cool. Jackie's story is one that should be told and retold, especially to young African-American adults who have given up hope. He is an inspiration."

"Amen. Anyway, I was thinking it would be nice to introduce you to some of the movers and shakers of Flamingo Beach and the neighboring towns. You might even meet an interesting man or two. If someone comes across your path that's interesting, Barry can fill you in."

"Okay, you've talked me into it. I accept."

Eileen stood. "Our lunch hour is over. I'll touch base with you in a week just to firm things up."

"Great. It'll be fun to meet some new people and see something of the neighboring towns as well."

"Hopefully you won't be too disappointed."

Jen doubted she would be. So far there was a lot about North Florida she liked.

Chapter 13

His mother was slowly driving him crazy and she'd only been there two days. Tre had come home from running a few errands expecting to find Marva lounging around the pool where she'd taken up residence. Instead, he'd found photos of women strewn over his dining room table.

"What are these?" he asked.

"Oh, those. Those are the women who applied for the position of Mrs. Monroe."

He gritted his teeth and ground out, "I didn't realize you had a contest going on. I don't mean to be difficult, but as I've said a hundred times I am perfectly capable of choosing my own bride."

"Are you? Then what's taking you so long?"

"I have a career that may not be to the likings of the average woman."

"Who said you needed average?" Marva came back with.

Good point! Whoever she was could not be average, not with the hours he kept or the persistent women constantly trailing him. Even so, his mother needed to stay out of it.

"Would you mind cleaning up a bit?" He gestured to the table. "Why don't you just dump the lot in the trash?"

Marva stuck out her lower lip. "I can't do that." There hadn't been any mention of her illness since she'd arrived nor had he seen her swallow one pill. He had the feeling he'd been conned big-time.

"Suit yourself but those women are bound to lose interest when no one responds, so you're just hauling around unnecessary trash."

"I've responded to them all."

"You've what?"

Now it was his blood pressure that was shooting sky-high.

"Someone had to answer the women before they got away."

"And that someone was you." Tre inhaled a breath before gritting out, "What exactly did you say?"

Marva smiled, proud that she'd taken things in hand. "I thanked them for their interest, asked for their phone numbers, and told them you'd be contacting them in the next week or so."

"You did not."

"I did, too."

The anger he'd worked so hard to control was back. It came in red furious waves, consuming him. He wanted to punch a hole in the wall, kick that table and its offensive contents right through the French door, over the balcony and into the ocean. He did none of that.

Breathe! Breathe! Breathe! Redirect your anger, think of something pleasant. Something you enjoy.

He would go for a run on the boardwalk until he calmed down. Tre headed for the bedroom to change clothes. He had swapped with another DJ and had the evening off.

Marva's voice came at him. "I thought we were going to dinner, baby."

"After I get back. It'll give you time to get rid of that rubbish."

"How am I going to know who's who when these

women e-mail me back?" she whined. "How are you going to know who you're taking to dinner?"

Tre stopped at the threshold of his bedroom. "I'm not taking anyone to dinner except someone of my own choosing."

"But there are three I've already invited to go out with you."

"Then uninvite them."

"I can't. I signed your name."

"Then find a good excuse to get me out of it!"

Tre entered his bedroom and kicked at the laundry basket. The receptacle flew across the room, spewing its contents onto the bamboo floor. Two days of Marva and he'd be signing up for anger management classes again. Twelve more days of her would turn him into an alcoholic.

He headed out the door.

An hour later he was huffing and puffing, having run his anger off. Every muscle and sinew felt it, but at least his head was clear. He'd soared past euphoria and gotten to the point where nothing mattered.

Why expend a lot of hateful energy on an old lady that he actually loved? Marva wasn't that old to begin with—fifty-nine was considered young today. He'd go home, apologize and take her to dinner. His mother's heart was in the right place.

As Tre dragged himself back to the apartment, Jen—outfitted in sneakers, running shorts, and T-back shirt—headed his way. He slowed down, jogging in place, waiting for her to catch up.

"Hey, I didn't know you ran," he greeted.

Jen now matched his pace exactly. "There's a lot you don't know about me," she huffed, smiling to take the vinegar off her words.

"Ah, but I plan on finding out."

Tre hadn't seen Jen since their dinner. Those memorable kisses still lingered, kisses that had left him wanting more. Much, much more.

"How about we run together sometime later this week?" he threw out.

"Knock on my door and if I'm home I'll join you," she said, preparing to jog on.

"I'll bring my mother by to meet you," he shouted over his shoulder.

She was several feet up the boardwalk when she called to him, "Okay. Something to look forward to." Then she waved and moved on.

Their encounter was entirely too brief. He'd have to remedy that shortly, and jogging would be the perfect excuse to get them together. The month had flown by and he wasn't any closer to getting her into bed. During that time he'd decided he wanted more than a quick hit. This was one woman he wanted to get to know.

Jen St. George was the type of woman that stimulated Tre on a lot of different levels. She was exciting, intriguing and far from bowled over by him. Plus she challenged his intelligence. That could make for a sweeter chase and a more satisfying capture. Nothing that came too easily was ever worth it.

Still thinking about Jen, Tre entered the building and got on the elevator. He was much calmer and more level-headed now. He was even looking forward to taking his mother out.

"Ma, where are you?" Tre called, noticing how quiet the apartment seemed.

No answer. But at least his dining room table was clear now and the damning evidence of his mother's meddling was gone. Maybe Marva was taking a walk.

Tre hopped into the shower, got out and quickly got dressed. He returned to the living room to find his mother still missing and now grew concerned. When another fifteen minutes went by and she still hadn't returned, he decided to go in search of her.

He wasted another half an hour wandering around the complex asking the residents if they'd seen Marva. Tre even quizzed the security guard behind the desk but, so far, nothing.

All the tension he'd worked off returned. He became even more concerned. Better head back to the apartment to see if Marva had called. Not that she would even remember he had a cell phone.

As Tre walked by Ida Rosenstein's apartment, the door opened, and his mother came through.

"Mother," Tre said, "I've been looking all over for you. I've been worried."

"Nothing to worry about," she said coolly, looking at him as if he'd lost his mind. "Ida and I have been catching up. I took her up on her previous offer of Rob Roys and we got to talking." She'd had more than one as her silly smile confirmed. "So when will I be meeting 5C?"

Ida was at the door now, the inevitable lit cigarette in hand. She was carrying her purse. "Where are you taking us to, young man?"

Marva had apparently extended the dinner invitation to Ida.

"Wherever you lovely ladies would like to go," Tre answered, glad that Ida would be there to provide a buffer.

"Charlie's," Ida piped up. "They have the best lobster in town and the freshest rolls."

And the most inflated prices.

"All right, ladies, you talked me into it." He held

out his arms to the women and they hooked their hands through the crooks.

All night Tre suffered through Ida's overly loud conversation and his mother's incessant quizzing. He suffered through the stories of indigestion, fading eyesight and crippling arthritis. Both ladies apparently forgot about their digestive ailments as they worked their way through a four-course meal. Tre even spotted Ida folding up the rolls in a napkin and shoving them in her purse.

He was halfway through his veal when an attractive young woman with a swishing ponytail and a skimpy skirt that barely covered her butt came over.

"Aren't you D'Dawg?" she asked.

"Who wants to know?" Ida squawked, saving him the effort of answering.

The invader shot her a sour look. "I'm talking to him not you."

"You're very disrespectful, young lady," Marva yelled, making her presence known. "What is it you want with my son?"

The young woman's demeanor immediately changed. "Ooohh, you're his mother? I was hoping he'd autograph my stomach." She flipped up her cropped top and handed Tre a felt-tipped pen.

"He will do no such thing. Cover yourself, young

lady." Marva slid a paper napkin forward. "Use this if you must."

The mini commotion had gotten the attention of the nearby tables. Tre recognized several of the patrons, one in particular he knew from running into her at several functions. She had a big position at *The Chronicle*. Tre quickly signed the napkin and slid it across the table.

The groupie read his words, and squealed, delighted at his personalized wording.

"I saw your ad on the Internet. At least I thought it might be yours, described you perfectly. I applied," she said between squeals.

"We're having dinner," Marva reminded her, quickly, too quickly. "Do you mind?"

He'd deal with his mother later.

The woman tossed Marva another sour look and then quickly covered with a smile when Tre stared at her.

"I'm sorry to have bothered you," the fan said, clutching the napkin to her chest. Her eyes never leaving Tre's, she quickly backed away.

"Lordie, does this happen often?" his mother asked, bug-eyed. "No wonder you're soured on women."

"I am not soured, Mother. We've been through this and we'll deal with the other issue when I get home."

What was the point in arguing or making a bigger scene than had already been created? His mother would believe what she wanted to believe. She'd thought he was gay.

The woman he'd recognized previously, the one who worked for *The Flamingo Beach Chronicle*, stopped by on her way out. She was accompanied by a distinguished graying man. Tre assumed he was her husband. That was soon confirmed when she introduced them.

"Eileen Brown," she reminded Tre. "I thought I recognized you but wasn't sure. When that fan approached I knew for sure."

"You're with *The Chronicle?*"

Eileen handed him her card. "Yes, I'm the advertising manager. Will you be at the reception the new African-American Library's throwing?"

Tre vaguely remembered getting an invitation. "Sure I'll go, but I may not be able to make the show. I'll come to the reception afterward. There is a reception? Right?"

"What's this about an African-American Library?" Marva asked. "And a reception?"

Eileen hurriedly explained.

"I'd like to go," Marva said, speaking up. "*The Jackie Robinson Story* should be good entertainment.

Besides, it's for a good cause and it would be my op-portunity to meet some of your friends."

"What about me?" Ida inquired in her too-loud voice. "Am I chopped liver?"

Dutifully Tre extended the invitation to both ladies. He hadn't planned on attending and had stashed his invitation somewhere. He'd have to find it. "I have to work but I'll be by later. I'll arrange for a car to pick you up and drop you off at the library. I'll drive you home myself."

"I have a license," Ida croaked. "I can drive."

Like hell he would let her.

"See you there then," Eileen said, deciding it was probably in her best interest to disappear. She inclined her head at the ladies and took her husband's hand.

"You do need my help," Marva said, the moment Eileen and her husband left. She grimaced. "If that young woman who came over earlier, is a reflection of what this town has to offer, heaven help us."

"I do *not* need your help, Mother. Please butt out and make sure that ad is off the Internet tonight."

"I took it off. Didn't I tell you that? She must have printed it out and held on to it." Marva sniffed. "I would never consider her anyway. She's not your type."

Ida's head ping-ponged. She curiously assessed the situation. "Tre doesn't need your help," she said, chortling. "5C's got him whipped. Just wait until you see her."

"Ida! Stop it!" Tre snapped.

The old lady cupped her ear. "What did you say?"

What was the use? He'd been ganged up on. He was wasting his breath. Nothing he said would make much difference. But he did plan on finding which site his mother had used and he was going to make sure that ad was off. He couldn't afford to have anyone think he was desperate.

Chapter 14

Just when she'd thought it was over with, and the topic of *Dear Jenna* old news, it started up again.

At Chere's urging, on their way to Pelican Island, and the African-American Library function, Jen tuned the radio into WARP. The tunes played tonight were some of her favorites: Mariah Carey, Beyoncé, Usher; an eclectic mix. They helped the twenty-minute trip to pass quickly.

Chere had more or less invited herself to come along. Jen was beginning to think that might have been a mistake. Her pushy assistant, with her loud ways and questionable manners was not what you'd expect at a highbrow social gathering.

The pesky DJ was on the air, his soulful voice reaching out to draw his audience in. Jen, hearing her moniker mentioned a time or two, tuned in to what he was saying.

"And just when we thought we'd heard enough of *Dear Jenna* and that hoagie column of hers," D'Dawg said, "*The Southern Tribune* hires this guy calling himself the *Love Doctor.* So ya know this on-air personality had to find out what's up with that. I did a little checking on him, just to make sure he wasn't a fraud. Guess what? The brother checked out. He's got degrees from Columbia and Cornell. So I'm thinking I bring him on the show, up against *Dear Jenna.* That should make for a lively debate. Watcha think of my idea, Flamingo Beach?"

The calls starting coming one after the other.

"Bring it on," one homeboy said.

"So what's this doc supposed to do for that ailing Southern paper?"

"Provide a cure," D'Dawg rasped, laughing at his own joke.

"More like put a Band-Aid on," another caller offered.

"Shit! What you going do now?" Chere's elbow

to the ribs brought Jen immediately back to the present. It caused Jen to swerve almost into the next lane. A horn blasted.

"My going up against the doctor might be good for circulation," Jen answered. "The PR can only help sell papers."

"Well, you handled yourself well the last time around. You put that man in his place. I wonder if that brother's single."

"What brother?" Jen asked, hoping she hadn't missed her exit. She'd printed out the directions to the library from Mapquest and had been trying to follow them diligently.

"*The Southern Chronicle*'s doctor," Chere explained, letting out a loud yawn. "Man, I'm hungry."

"I'm sure you'll find out." Jen made a sharp right, and then a left and followed a winding road.

"We're here," she announced, pulling up in front of a clapwood building that looked like it might have been replicated from plans from another era. The landscaping though charming was organized chaos. Hibiscus bushes jockeyed for position with bougainvillea, ixora, birds of paradise and trailing ferns.

They followed a number of people up the croton-lined pathway and toward the stained-glass front door. Already a sizeable crowd spilled from the lobby. Voices were animated as guests greeted friends and acquaintances.

Jen looked around for Eileen. She hadn't had time to warn the advertising and marketing manager that Chere would be her date this evening. But Eileen and her husband were nowhere in sight, they were probably already seated.

Jen glanced at her tickets. The layout of the auditorium was a mystery to her and ushers were not visible. "We should go and find our seats," she suggested. "We can mingle afterwards at the reception."

They finally found an usher who led them to their row. As Chere heaved her bulk into the too-small seat she loudly whispered, "I hope whoever's playing Jackie Robinson's fine, if not it's going be hell sitting for two hours while my butt's asleep."

"Sssshhh!"

It would be a losing battle trying to keep Chere quiet and entertained for a couple of hours. With any luck her irrepressible admin assistant would fall asleep.

Tre heard the raised voices even from the parking lot. The patrons inside the building seemed to be having a good time. The reception must be going well and the drinks flowing.

He circled several times and finally, exasperated, parallel parked the radio station van illegally. Maybe the cops would have mercy on him when they spotted the station logo on the side of the vehicle. Pelican Island, with its sparse population could use all the publicity it could get, and so could the new African-American Library. No one had to know he wasn't there in a journalist's capacity.

Tre had come straight from the station and hadn't had time to change. When he'd left for work that evening, he'd worn dress pants, skipping his usual jeans. He'd remembered to bring a sports jacket with him as well. Knowing the Porsche would never accommodate both his mother and Ida, he'd had a car service he sometimes used pick up the ladies. He'd borrowed one of WARP's vehicle's to transport them back.

After stepping out of the van he shrugged into the lightweight linen jacket. It had been at least a year since he'd had the need to wear a jacket, and only because someone at the station had gotten married and invited him.

Tre hoped that unsupervised his mother and Ida had managed to conduct themselves in an appropriate manner. He wasn't expecting perfect behavior; that would be too much from them. Just behavior that most people would attribute to senior citizens and easily forgive.

Tre's first impressions as he entered the lobby were of a reception going extremely well. A huge crowd milled around the four bars, taking advantage of the free drinks. Waiters hired by the catering company circled, bearing trays of canapés that were immediately scooped up when people converged from everywhere. A quick glance around the room yielded no sign of his mother or Ida.

Hoping to blend in, Tre eased his way into the midst of chaos. He headed for a bar that seemed less crowded than the rest. He would have just one drink because he was driving. As he fought his way against a steady stream of traffic, a palm clapped his back.

"Aren't you Tre Monroe, the DJ?"

He was tempted to lie but what would be the point? These high-profile events attracted the movers and shakers of Flamingo Beach and the surrounding neighborhoods. This might very well be someone to get to know.

Tre stuck out his hand. The man clasped it and shook it vigorously. "Bernard Cain, I've enjoyed your show immensely, especially what you've done with it the last three weeks."

Tre thanked Bernard and prepared to move on but

the man wasn't done. "It will be interesting to have *Dear Jenna* up against Doctor Fraser. Both have very distinctive styles."

"Have you met them?" Tre asked.

"Earlier on I was introduced to Dr. Fraser. He's the guy dressed in a pinstriped suit. He doesn't look anything like you would picture a doctor. You know what I mean." He smiled.

No, Tre didn't know what he meant, but now his interest was piqued.

Bernard was off and running. "I haven't met *Dear Jenna* but it's rumored she's here, too."

Tre perked up immediately. It would be interesting to meet the woman he poked fun at face-to-face.

"Who would know if she's here?" he asked.

"Probably someone on the planning committee. Excuse me, I have to go say hi to someone." And just like that Bernard was gone.

Tre prodded and pushed his way to a line that snaked around the corner. As he waited to get closer to a drink, he gazed around the room trying to see who was who.

Mayor Rabinowitz was holding court with some official-looking types who might or might not be from the city. Some of the small business owners who advertised on WARP were nursing drinks while chatting amongst themselves. He caught a glimpse of a woman who looked very much like his attractive neighbor but he could not imagine what she would be doing here. He'd thought she was a professional woman but he'd not thought her contacts would be this far-reaching.

Now he definitely needed that drink. Tre looked over in the direction of the corner where the woman who looked like Jen stood. She was talking to a man in a pinstriped suit while a woman, who could well stand to go on a diet, hovered. The woman looked slightly out of place in the midst of a group that was conservatively dressed. His mother and Ida were still nowhere to be seen.

Ten minutes later Tre was finally face-to-face with the bartender. He played it safe and ordered a beer. It would be thirst-quenching and something to hold in his hands as he made the rounds. He again circled the room hoping to run into his mother and Ida.

"You looking for me?" The heavyset woman who'd been part of Jen's group was practically in his face. She wore a sparkly outfit and sandals with rhinestones, and ridiculous curls bounced around her face. The entire getup was way too youthful for a woman in her thirties and she stood out like a beacon in a sea of tailored suits.

"Actually I'm looking for my mother and her friend," Tre answered politely, trying to hide his smile. He was cataloging all of his impressions so that he could share them on tomorrow's show.

"Maybe I can help find them. What do they look like?"

The offer was appreciated, but suspect. Tre described Ida and Marva.

"Oh, those two." The woman chortled as if enjoying a private joke. Tre thought he might have run into her at another function but they'd never been introduced. "The last I saw they were putting away the drinks. I overheard one of them say to that woman over there—" she pointed in the direction of the back of a woman's head "—that she should try an Internet site called Café Singles. What would those two know about Internet dating?"

Oh. God! Tell him they weren't at it.

"Where are they now?"

His companion shrugged massive shoulders. Every inch of flesh wobbled. "Who knows? I'm Chere Adams, by the way. You here with anyone?"

"Nice to meet you, Chere," Tre said politely, because what else was there to say. "I better go find my mother and her friend." Off he wandered before the woman settled herself in for the night.

Tre stopped to exchange greetings with some people who recognized him. He shook hands and fended off a few of the women's flirtatious advances. At last he spotted Ida and Marva giggling while talking to the rod-thin man in the pinstriped suit. Noting each held two drinks in hand, he made his way over.

"Hello, Mother, Ida," Tre greeted, inserting himself between the three people.

"Hello, son," Marva enthused, her pitch matching Ida's on a particularly bad day when her hearing aid failed her. Marva seldom called him "son." Must be the alcohol talking.

"About time you arrived," Ida said, tossing back what remained in her glass. "Have you met the doctor? He's new in town."

Tre nodded, quickly putting two and two together. So this was probably *The Southern Tribune*'s new hire. He looked a lot like Chris Rock, the stand-up comedian, except he was a lot thinner, actually to the point of being emaciated.

The doctor's hair was cropped so short that portions of his scalp shone through. His Ghandi-style glasses, more popular in the seventies than today, gave him a mad-scientist look, and the scruffy mustache covering his upper lip did nothing to improve his appearance. When he smiled, a perfect set of capped teeth sparkled.

"Doctor Allen Fraser," he said, sticking out his hand.

"Tre Monroe." No need to elaborate further. Tre's mission now was to get Ida and Marva home before they embarrassed themselves and him. He and the doc could discuss business over a phone call. "Ladies, ready to go home?" Tre inquired.

"What?" Ida yelped. "I can't hear you." Her hearing came and went conveniently, it seemed.

"No, we are not ready," Marva answered in a more strident tone. "We're just starting to mingle."

"You must be getting tired," Tre implored. "I know I am. I'll be happy to see my bed."

A bewildered Dr. Fraser looked from one woman to another.

Ida's old eyes sparkled. "Uh-huh. The night's just begun. You wouldn't believe who's here." She pointed to a spot across the room before lowering her voice an octave. "Our sexy neighbor in 5C, the one you're hot for. I introduced Marva, right, Marva? Tre, run off and chat her up before some stud moves in."

Tre wanted to clap his hands against both sides of his head. He could only imagine what havoc the unchaperoned twosome might have caused. This could easily require damage repair.

"Are you speaking of Jen St. George?" the bespectacled doctor interjected. He had to have been following the conversation all along. Even his tone sounded pompous.

Tre took a hit of beer directly from the bottle. "You two know each other?"

"No, we just met. Fascinating woman. Very good at what she does." The doctor looked over his shoulder as if he didn't want to be overheard, then turned back to them.

"Look at how far she's come and in just a few months. Her name is on every citizen's tongue."

Tre's instincts had been right all along. His next-door neighbor must be a high-powered attorney who'd just settled a lucrative case. He would do research on her the first opportunity he got. So far the doctor was proving to be a veritable wealth of information.

"Dr. Fraser," a woman called from behind them. "I just wanted to say, welcome to Flamingo Beach. I can't wait to read your column."

Banalities were exchanged. Tre saw it as the perfect opportunity to move Ida and his mother along. But the pair had already slipped off somewhere.

"Dammit!"

Fifteen minutes later, Tre worked his way around the room a second time. He'd not encountered the slick twosome and concluded that they liked it that way. During his second round, he'd run into his boss, Boris Schwartz and Boris's significant other, a hot-looking woman from the Philippines. The three had exchanged trivial cocktail patter. Not wanting to take up any more of their time, Tre had excused himself and gone on his way.

"Well, fancy seeing you here," a cultured female voice called as he was scanning the room for signs of Ida and Marva.

Tre thought he recognized that voice. He'd been expecting to bump into Jen eventually. He spun around, surprised to find her in the company of Eileen and Barry Brown.

Eileen gaped. Her tongue practically touched the floor.

"You know each other?"

"Yes, we do." Jen laid a playful hand on Tre's forearm. "Trestin and I live in the same building. He's my noisy next-door neighbor."

"Too funny. You've been holding out on me, Jen," Eileen said. "Who would think you and D'Dawg lived in the same building? It just goes to show you, you can separate the professional from the personal."

"D'Dawg?" Jen stared at him.

"My radio personality," Tre said smoothly because

what else was there to say. "Didn't I tell you I was in communications?"

The enormity of it all took a while to sink in. What a set he had. The balls of him to stand there acting all cavalier.

"Yes, you did mention something like that," she managed, conscious of Eileen and Barry's interest. "I guess I just wasn't listening closely and didn't put two and two together."

Jen forced herself to keep a smile on her face, and her hand on his forearm, while her next-door neighbor, the bane of her existence, looked down at her with sultry, brown bedroom eyes.

She wanted to slap that grin off his face. He'd made a fool of her.

And she'd make sure she let him know just how upset she was. Big-time. Just wait until she got him alone!

Chapter 15

This was the infamous D'Dawg, the man who'd put her reputation at risk and attacked her credibility. To think he lived right next door to her.

Now Jen understood the loud music, the posturing, the strange hours and the groupies at his door. No, she wasn't being fair. There had also been a kind, caring side to him, hidden behind all that bluster. She'd even begun to like the man.

"Life is strange, isn't it?" Eileen continued with a bemused expression on her face. "Here the two of you are at each other's... Ouch."

"Sorry, awfully clumsy of me."

Jen removed her high heel off of Eileen's instep. She hadn't meant to step on her colleague's foot that hard. But at least it had shut her up, and that was Jen's goal.

Knowledge was power. Jen now knew of Trestin's other persona but he still didn't know she was *Dear Jenna*. Therefore she had the upper hand. She planned on keeping it that way for as long as possible.

"So that's why you kept your career a secret," she gushed and playfully punched his arm. All the while her insides roiled and a red-hot anger consumed her. He'd lied all along, pretending he didn't know about the controversy and didn't listen to the D'Dawg show. He didn't listen, he *was* the show. "I can't believe I live next door to someone famous."

Eileen wisely kept her counsel, looking from one to the other. She'd gotten the message loud and clear.

"I've never considered myself famous," Tre graciously said, "I'm just doing what I've always done, entertain people. Some appreciate my unique brand of humor. Some do not."

"You do a good job. I love your show and I especially enjoyed the way you poked fun at *Dear Jenna*. What was it you called her?"

"Aunt Jemima!" Chere, who'd returned from the

bathroom and must have been listening carefully, supplied. If nothing else, she caught on quickly. She was streetwise and smart and hopefully would keep her mouth shut.

"You're 'the dog,'" she said loudly. "Oops! I mean the on-air personality, the man who couldn't find his mama."

Tre nodded. "Yes, as a matter of fact I'm still looking for her."

Chere pointed a golden nail in the direction of the ladies' room. "Your mama and that loud senior citizen are in the bathroom. Want me to get them for you?"

Tre looked exasperated. Jen actually felt sorry for him. During their last dinner he'd alluded to the fact his mother was a handful.

"Yes, please. It's bedtime for them. I'll come with you." He nodded goodbye to Jen and the Browns and plodded after Chere.

"You didn't know he was D'Dawg, did you?" Eileen said when Tre was well out of earshot.

"No, I didn't have a clue."

Eileen lowered her voice confidentially, "You do realize he's interested in you."

"No, he's not."

Denial was safe. But even as Jen shook her head

she remembered his searing kisses and her passionate reaction to them.

How could something like this have happened? She'd sworn off men, wanted nothing to do with them. Didn't trust them period, especially after Anderson.

"What are you going to do about him?" Eileen asked while Barry, her husband, maintained a poker face and offered no comment.

What was she going to do about Trestin now that she knew who he was? Eventually he would find out she was *Dear Jenna*. Any comfortable rapport they'd established would quickly come to an end. Meanwhile she could have fun with him. She just had to make sure her heart was protected in the process. A woman could only stand so much hurt.

"Mother," Tre said, two days later as they rode in the Porsche. "Is Café Singles the site you posted on?"

"Why are you asking?" Marva pretended to fumble for something in her purse.

"No particular reason."

He'd decided to take his mother with him to the grand opening of a new car dealership. D'Dawg was the featured celebrity and Miriam Young, "the Flip-Flop Momma," Mayor Rabinowitz's competition, was supposed to show up.

With the election now less than a week away, things were heating up. Today, because it was a weekend, the new Ford dealership expected a record turnout. Marva had wanted to accompany him, claiming she wanted to see him in action doing his disk jockey thing. She was especially fascinated by Miriam Young, the feisty single parent willing to shake up the old boys.

The convertible's roof was down and a balmy breeze blew through the interior. Tre, sensing Marva was avoiding conflict, pushed a little.

"You placed an advertisement on a dating site on my behalf. I asked you to remove it and I want to make sure you did."

Marva sniffed. She could turn the waterworks on and off when it was convenient. "I told you I canceled it. Why don't you believe me?"

"I'm just trying to avoid any further embarrassing incidents. I have a reputation to maintain, Mother. I can't afford to come off as desperate and needing my mother to find me a mate." Tre took his eyes off the road momentarily. "Hopefully I've convinced you I'm not gay."

Marva cackled. "You did. What's happening with 5C?"

"We've been out a couple of times."

That's all she needed to know and that was all he planned on telling her.

"And?"

"And nothing, Mother. She's an interesting woman and a beautiful one."

"Yes, I picked that up. Even the mouthpiece down the hall thinks so."

"Mouthpiece?"

"Camille Lewis."

In the short time she'd been there, Marva sure managed to get around.

They pulled into a space at the Ford dealership. Tre helped his mother out of the front seat then made sure he got the crate holding the CDs and autographed photos he was going to give away, out of the trunk.

The radio station's van was already parked, and Bill, the assistant producer, had set up the wheel of fortune. They would be giving away the CDs, photographs and other promotional items to a few lucky winners. Overhead a large orange blimp floated. The words WARP Celebrates The Opening Of Ferris Ford were emblazoned in purple. You couldn't miss the blimp. The orange against a blue sky with puffy white clouds was an eye-catcher.

"I have to get to work, Mother," Tre said. "There's complimentary refreshments over there, plus the local vendors are giving out samples of products. You can even get free newspapers. Both *The Tribune* and *Chronicle* are on the premises. Try not to get into trouble."

"I want to see the Flip-Flop Momma, hear what she has to say."

With a wave of her hand, Marva was off, wending her way toward the area where the vendors and a makeshift stage had been set up. Glad she seemed happy and occupied, Tre headed off to work.

Bill, his assistant producer, was a red-haired kid with freckles and an optimistic attitude.

"Hey, Tre," he greeted. "We've already had several women by to see you. I told them you were running late. The box with the drawing for that Fun Ship cruise is full, you might want to empty it."

Tre removed the business cards and folded pieces of paper from the box. He stuffed them into an envelope Bill gave him. One of their sponsors, advertising themselves as the most popular cruise line in the world, had donated a cruise for two. That marketing move was driving quite a bit of business.

Word soon got out D'Dawg was there and people started to drift over. Tre pumped more hands than he cared to count and kissed ladies of every ethnic makeup. As he paused to take a sip of water, his thoughts turned to Jen. He'd been so busy entertaining his mother, and making sure she stayed out of trouble, he'd not followed through on his plans of seduction. The way he felt about her he wasn't sure seduction was now quite the right word.

Marva and Jen had somehow managed to meet without him introducing them. But he wanted to see for himself how they interacted. Both were strong personalities in totally different ways. Maybe what he needed to do was take them out for a day in the sun. His boat was moored at the Flamingo Beach public docks but he seldom had time to use it.

It was an indulgence, just like the Porsche was, but the speedboat was something he'd always wanted. Tre had purchased the boat secondhand, reasoning what was the point of living in a waterfront community if you didn't take advantage of all it had to offer?

He'd grown up poor in Detroit. He and his mother and brother had barely gotten by. Expensive cars and boats were luxuries seen only on television. Now it felt good to know that his hard work and ambition had paid off and that if he chose to, he could own things that he'd only been able to dream of. This was another reason buying the apartment was so important to him. Few members of his family were home owners.

"How's your mother?" a female voice brayed, pulling him out of his meanderings.

Tre looked up into the smiling face of the haystack he'd encountered the other night at the library. He searched his memory. Chere something-or-other.

"Chere Adams," she reminded him.

"My mother? She's around somewhere," he answered, gesturing toward the vendor area. "She wanted to hear Miriam Young." Dare he ask if her friend accompanied her? No, let her bring it up.

"So how do I enter this contest?" Chere asked, stabbing a finger at the cruise entry box.

"Put your business card in. If you don't have one—" he doubted she did "—write your name on this form." Tre shoved a slip of paper at her.

Chere Adams surprised him by removing a couple of business cards from her oversized rattan bag and flipping them into the box.

"Fix it so I win," she said shamelessly.

Tre winked at her. "Sure. But who you going take with you if you win?"

"My buddy."

"Your buddy got a name?"

Chere smiled provocatively. "She your next door neighbor. By the way, you still on Café Singles?"

"What?"

Another knowing smile followed. "Well your photo ain't posted if that's what you're worried about. But I read the profile and it seems pretty obvious to me."

He was going to kill his mother, murder her with his bare hands.

"I don't know what you're talking about," Tre denied.

"Sure you do. Your mama wrote to *Dear Jenna* about you when she thought you were gay." Busted! The woman was a heck of a lot smarter than he gave her credit for, and downright shrewd, too. "Hmmmm. Wonder if my buddy knows you're on a dating site? Maybe I should tell her."

"Now don't you do that."

"Why not?"

A flurry of activity behind the Adams woman got his attention. Five or six teenyboppers clutching the pictures Bill was giving out at the entrance, advanced.

"D'Dawg! Oh, my God!"

"Tre Monroe. You're my idol. I love you."

"I just want to touch you, D'Dawg."

"I want to have your baby."

Chere burst out laughing. "Looks like you're busy. I'll make room for your fan club. Make sure I win."

She clomped off on platform shoes that looked wicked. Tre's attention now turned to the squealing teenagers who were jumping up and down. The next half an hour passed quickly.

There were fifteen minutes left before he could pack up. Now the crowd had thinned considerably. Tre spotted his mother toddling toward him. She looked exhausted and was laden down by bags filled with freebies. So far there was still not one word about high blood pressure or out-of-control diabetes.

Tre pulled out the chair Bill had vacated. "Here, Mother, take a seat."

Marva sank into it gratefully. "You want to see what I got? I can't wait to get back to Detroit and show Mrs. Calhoun how Florida parties."

He couldn't wait, either. "Later, Mother, later. As soon as Bill gets back we'll take off."

Marva wasn't listening. She pulled a fanny pack out of one of the bags and held it up. "I got this for Ida."

"That was thoughtful of you."

A T-shirt with a wild beach scene followed. The front of the shirt read *Ride The Wave With The Flamingo Beach Chronicle*.

"And this is what that nice girl from 5C gave to me," Marva chortled. "Now wasn't that sweet?"

"Jen gave you the shirt?" Tre asked, his curiosity getting the better of him. "She's here?"

"Yes, we were standing together listening to

Miriam Young talk about her platform. Afterward she handed it to me."

"You get along with 5C?" Tre asked, surprising himself by holding his breath while waiting for her answer.

"Oh, yes, very much so. I think she's perfect for you. She'd keep you on your toes. By the way, I smoothed the way for you. I told her you were interested. The ball's in your court, son. Don't drop it."

Chapter 16

"Tre asked me to go out on his boat," Jen said to Chere later that week when they were working at home. There was no point in keeping it a secret. Chere already knew they'd been out a time or two; they'd even been jogging together. The minute Jen stepped foot on Tre's boat it would be all over town anyway.

"Interesting," Chere offered, looking up from the pile of letters she was going through. She wore rhinestone harlequin glasses that made her look like a well-fed cat. "I wonder what he's up to."

"You are suspicious? I'm rubbing off on you." Jen

took that opportunity to stand and stretch. She'd been hunched over a computer for way too long. "And I told him I would provide the eats."

"Generous of you. You know he's on Café Singles?"

For a beat too long, Jen stared out the window and onto an angry-looking bay. White-crested waves tossed little sailboats around and the sky above was heavy with storm clouds. It was too early for hurricanes but not too early for the afternoon rains that came and went as quickly as they began.

"Where have I heard the name before?" Jen asked. "What is it anyway?"

"The most popular site for African-Americans looking to get hooked up."

"And you're on it?"

Chere smiled enigmatically.

A wicked idea was beginning to formulate in Jen's mind. "Log onto the site. Let me take a look."

"Jen, you're up to no good."

"I am?"

She knew her smile was positively wicked. She was enjoying this.

Chere found Café Singles and quickly entered using a password.

"As I thought," Jen said. "You're already a member."

Chere's smile matched hers. "Well, a girl can't

sit home these days and wait for men to come calling." She scrolled through a number of profiles
then brought up the one she thought was Tre's.
"Here he is."

Taking her time, Jen read thoughtfully. "Well, it
certainly sounds like him," she announced after she
was through.

"So what's next? You got a digital photo?"
Chere asked.

"Sure thing. I have my *Dear Jenna* photo."

Chere's eyes went wide. "Puh-lease, not that ugly
old thing with you wearing that zoot suit."

"That's the one I'm using."

With that Chere began laughing so hard she was
actually hiccupping. In a joint effort they uploaded the
photo. "That boy's going be mad when he finds out.
How you going to sign your e-mail, Aunt Jemima?"
Chere dissolved in laughter again, her double chins
bobbing.

"I just might." Leaning over her assistant's shoulders, Jen began typing. Before she could change her
mind she hit the send button.

"Let's get back to work, shall we?" she said, no
sooner had Chere hoisted herself off the chair.

"I'll be back as soon as I find something to eat in

your refrigerator. Just looking at that stack of letters is enough to make me hungry."

With that Chere waddled off.

Now it was wait and see if Marva got her message.

Sunday turned out to be the perfect day for boating. Tre, after checking in with Jen, asked if she minded taking his mother with her down to the docks. He planned on getting there earlier to make sure the Chris Craft was clean and ready to go. He'd hired a deckhand to clean the boat thoroughly but without close supervision one never knew.

Satisfied the work had been completed, Tre stood at the entrance of the public dock waiting for his mother and Jen to arrive. Initially he'd had some trepidation about leaving the two alone but then he'd figured his mother had already been in Jen's company unsupervised, so whatever damage had been done would have occurred even before.

While waiting, Tre examined his real reasons for throwing the two together. He'd wanted to see for himself how Marva and Jen got along. He'd been toying with the idea of pursuing 5C, and not just for the seduction he'd initially planned. Almost overnight it had struck him that this was exactly the kind of woman he was looking for. Jen was serious but had a playful side to her. She seemed outgoing and capable of handling herself, yet at the same time vulnerable, and there was an element of mystery that surrounded her. He wanted to unravel that mystery.

The Miata pulled into a vacant spot. Jen raced from the driver's side and came around to help his mother out. Jen was dressed for boating, wearing white shorts and a black-and-white T-shirt. A jaunty red sailor hat covered hair that had been pulled back into a ponytail. White sneakers and black socks, the kind with the pom-poms peeking over the back, completed the look.

His mother, though more covered up, went with the tropical theme. She was wearing a wild-looking thing that he'd seen ladies in Hawaii wear during luaus. Her wide-brimmed hat had colorful flowers that bobbed when she spoke. And she was speaking a mile a minute, as she usually did.

Tre waved to them as they began approaching the docks. He could see his mother's expression clearly now and a beaming smile wreathed her face. He exhaled a breath. The two were getting along quite well. He also noticed the picnic basket Jen carried, the one she'd promised to bring.

Tre greeted his ladies with a kiss on each cheek. His mother wore the heavy fragrance that she always did, and Jen smelled like citrus.

"*Noir* is anchored at the far dock," he announced. "Are you ladies up for the walk?"

"Sure," his mother puffed. He noticed she had twined an arm through Jen's. The two were as thick as thieves.

"Can I help you with that?" Tre was already wrestling Jen for the basket's handle.

She relinquished it. Mindful that his mother was not exactly a lightweight, and getting up there in age, they meandered slowly toward the boat.

The rented deckhand that most of the community used had finished hosing down the deck and polishing the chrome. The boat sparkled invitingly under the sun.

"Oh, my lord," Marva said, bringing a plump hand to her heart. "You've made it, boy."

"I'm not quite there yet." Tre kept his expression bland but was secretly delighted at his mother's joy. It felt good to know she was proud of him. "I have bigger plans so I can get bigger toys."

"These seem pretty big to me."

Tre could not see Jen's expression because her eyes were hidden behind huge sunglasses. She waited until they were seated on the deck, his mother ensconced on the built-in bench at the back, and she in the front next to him to say, "Bigger plans. How much bigger can they get?"

He started up the boat, shouting over the noise of the motor. "I've always wanted to be on the air in New York City. It's been a dream of mine since I was a boy."

"You do think big. What's your plan to get there?"

They were slowly chugging out to the open bay, passing boats with families and singles out for a day of fun in the sun. Tre inhaled the smell of salt, loving it.

"I started off broadcasting during college," Tre began. Jen, all ears, listened intently. "Just the local college radio. It was fun, made me feel like a big man. And I was good at it. After I graduated I was lucky to get a job in a little town in Missouri. That lasted all of a year before I was fired. Since then, I've worked in backwater towns in Georgia and Louisiana. Then I hit the big time. I landed a job in Boston, cohosting a show."

"That's impressive. Boston's a big urban city, a quick shuttle flight to New York. Why didn't you stay?"

"Because I found that city just a bit too stuffy. Plus WARP came to me with this offer. It was an opportunity to have my own show and they made me an offer I couldn't refuse. They were already thinking ahead, anticipating the Northeast baby boomers would be buying homes on the Florida Coast and would miss a particular broadcasting style."

"So you're the answer to urban withdrawal. But didn't you tell me you were from Detroit?"

"He is," Marva chimed in from her throne in the back. She was tired of being silent. "A born and bred Michigan boy." How she'd heard the conversation over the noise of the motor was anyone's guess.

Jen shot Marva a dazzling white smile before turning back to him.

"And you, you still haven't told me what you do."

"I think I'll go keep your mother company for a while," was her answer as she slid off her chair. "Be back shortly."

Tre had been surprised that she'd not had a much stronger reaction to his radio persona when she'd found out. He hadn't expected her to fawn all over him but he had expected her to demand answers or at least accuse him of lying. Not that he'd lied outright. He'd just omitted a few essential details about his career. It occurred to him that Jen wasn't exactly forthcoming about her career either and he wondered what that was about.

All that could wait to be pondered later. It was a lovely day and he didn't plan on ruining it. Jen and Marva were getting along famously and his mother was not the easiest person in the world. In fact she could be downright cantankerous at times when the mood struck her.

Tre steered the boat into a secluded cove where there were picnic tables and benches and a small beach where people swam. Heron Bay was one of the better kept secrets in North Florida.

"We're here, ladies," he announced, slowing the boat down and angling it into the slip, preparing to drop anchor.

"Would you like help with that?" Jen asked. She'd already sprung up and jumped ashore before he could stop her. "Throw me that rope."

It surprised him how competent she was at tying the boat to the dock.

"Thank you. You make a good mate," he said jokingly after he'd helped Marva off.

"Yes, she does," his mother said, nodding enthusiastically.

They spent the day walking around the small island and cooling off in the water when they got overly warm. Tre received an unexpected treat when Jen stripped down to a modest red bikini with red clasps holding the bottom and top together. He stopped himself one note short of a wolf whistle.

For a moment Jen's hazel eyes flashed, then she summoned a smile. "Was that a compliment?"

His mother for once kept her mouth shut. Her expression indicated she knew something they didn't. After a while they found a shady spot and devoured the contents of Jen's picnic basket.

"I think I'm going to take a nap," Marva said. She pointed a finger. "Right over there in that shady spot where they have lounge chairs you can rent."

"Good idea," Tre said, suddenly wanting to be alone with Jen. Although she had put her shorts back on, that little red bikini was beginning to get to him.

"You two have fun." Marva twiddled her fingers in their direction.

They set off down a path with a sign that said, Nature Walk. Tre pointed out some of the foliage and flora native to Florida. Jen looked at him curiously. "How come you know so much about all of this?" She gestured with two hands, the nails meticulously trimmed.

"Would you believe," he said, capturing one of those expansive hands in his, "that I was a botany major?"

"Get out."

"My minor was communications."

She frowned. "Now that's a puzzling combination."

"Not really. I wanted to be versatile and prepared for anything."

They'd come to a nature preserve. Flamingos, ibises and herons roamed freely.

"Boy, do I wish I'd brought my camera," Jen said, leaning over the railing separating humans from the birds.

"I have this," Tre offered, handing her his cell phone. "Modern technology makes all things possible."

She snapped a couple of shots and let him look at them.

"Not bad as digitals go."

They walked some more, this time admiring the caged panthers and a watery inlet which was supposedly alligator-infested, although none of the gators so much as raised their heads.

Wanting to relax, Tre sank onto a little wooden bench and patted the spot next to him.

"Are you thinking of making that purchase we spoke of?" he asked.

"You mean, buying the condo?"

"Yes, I heard there aren't that many left. The residents are snapping them up at the insiders' price."

"I suppose I should do something, and quickly."

"It will be a good investment. You can't lose, even if you decide not to stay."

She looked at him curiously. "I recently sold a house, packed up everything I owned and moved to

Flamingo Beach. I have no plans to go anywhere in a hurry."

"That must mean you like our little town," he said, his index finger taking on a life of its own, and touching the tip of her nose.

Jen wiggled her nose and smiled at him. "I do, although it took some getting used to. I mean Ashton was not exactly a big city. The Midwest is a pretty laid-back place and fairly accepting of pretty much everything and everyone. Flamingo Beach is…well…"

"The south?"

"Exactly. It seems mired in tradition. Here's a town where the majority of people are African-American yet people don't seem to mingle. You've got whites living on one side and blacks on the other."

"Except for our complex. Our residents seem to mingle peaceably. From what I understand it was the architect's vision to offer truly multicultural living."

"Ah, to realize a dream."

"You must have one," he insisted. "We all do."

"I do. Mine is to be completely self-sufficient."

"By that you mean you don't want a man in your life?"

Tre held his breath even as his hands wandered. His runaway fingers traced a path across her cheeks before floating downward to cup Jen's chin.

"No, by that I mean that I am never ever going to so totally fall in love that I lose sight of other important things in life."

"Like what?" Tre asked, leaning over and kissing her cheek. He twined his fingers through hers and forced her to look at him. Was that the glimmer of unshed tears in her eyes?

"Like my health and happiness and like remaining my own person," Jen said, and yes, those were real tears. "I'll always have a career because that's the only thing you'll have when it's over with."

"You've been hurt," he said matter-of-factly and kissed her. This time it wasn't a teasing kiss but one so passion-filled he was close to losing his head. Jen frustrated him with her secrecy. If only he could break down the barriers and get to know the woman a little bit. Would she let him?

And she was kissing him back with the same amount of intensity, letting their tongues meet and meld. The shrill cries of birds echoed in the background and wildlife called to each other in an intricate mating dance. The clasp that held the top of her bathing suit was only inches from his itching fingers. No, better not go there. But she was pressing into him and he felt her taut nipples against his chest. And, God it was tempting.

His mother…well, God only knew where she was. It was thoughts of her that kept him grounded and in control.

Tre's arms slid around Jen, his palm kneading the supple flesh of her back. Her skin was warmed by the sun and taut under his hand. Tre kissed her again, and then with every ounce of restraint he could muster put her away from him

"What—"

"We need to get back."

No, it was he who needed to get back and get himself in check. He didn't want to imagine what was going on in her head as he took her hand and they retraced their steps, heading back toward Marva.

His mother was still sprawled out on her lounger and looked like she had no intention of moving anytime soon. Thank God!

"I'll come by later," Tre whispered, "to finish what I started. Think you'll be home?"

"I'll be home," Jen answered.

But there was a look in her eye he wasn't sure how to interpret.

She'd better be home or he'd go clear out of his mind.

Chapter 17

Jen was just drifting off to sleep when she heard a sound at her front door. Faint at first, then a rapid staccato. Too much sun and frolicking in the ocean that day had left her feeling lethargic and sleepy.

It had been a great day and she'd enjoyed every moment of being with Tre and Marva. She'd seen that other side of Tre that she liked, the warm and caring side, considerate of his mother's feelings, and catering to their every need.

Jen had returned slightly sunburned. Her skin had a copper glow to it and her cheeks and shoulders were burned. She'd been full of chicken salad and avocado sandwiches. They'd washed them down with sweet tea then sampled the excellent white wine she'd brought along. Mangos and melons had been the fruit of choice for dessert.

And they'd talked and talked about their philosophies on life. Jen had finally concluded that the brash, flip loudmouth D'Dawg personality was just all an act. And she'd pretty much forgiven him for all the mean things he'd said about *Dear Jenna*.

During their alone time, Tre hadn't once mentioned Café Singles or *Dear Jenna* responding to his ad. Perhaps he just hadn't taken the response seriously. He had to know *Dear Jenna* was yanking his chain bigtime. The only question was would he retaliate?

Another insistent rap, then an inquiry. "Jen, are you up?"

This time Jen's eyes flew wide open. She hadn't been dreaming. Tre had mentioned something about stopping by later to finish what they had started. Now he was here to make good on his promise. She was a big girl, quite capable of making her own decisions. She knew what the consequences would be if they made the leap from next-door neighbors to lovers. What she needed to do was go into this with her eyes wide open but having no expectations.

Jen flipped off the covers, quickly ran a comb through her hair and found the wrapper she'd had difficulty finding the last time around.

"Hi," she greeted, opening the door just wide enough to stick her head out.

"I woke you. I'm sorry."

Trying to wipe the sleep away, she swiped at her eyes. "Not really."

"I'll let you get back to bed then."

"No, no. It's all right. I'm up. Come in."

She stood aside, making room for him to enter.

He was wearing a track suit that emphasized his arm and leg muscles. Sculptured and fit were what came to mind. You could tell he worked out. Jen had noticed that earlier when Tre had emerged from the boat's cuddy cabin wearing his swim trunks. He was now standing awkwardly in the middle of her living room.

"What time is it, anyway?" Jen asked, the watch she normally wore, left on the nightstand.

"A little after nine. I waited until Mother passed out before heading over."

They both knew why he'd waited for Marva to fall asleep and why he was there.

"How about a glass of wine, unless you'd prefer something else?" Jen asked.

"I'll take beer if you have it. Doesn't much matter the brand."

Jen got him his beer, poured herself a glass of wine and got nuts to snack on. When she returned, Tre was standing on the balcony looking down at the bay. She set down their drinks and the bowl of nuts on the table. The minute she straightened, Tre placed an arm around her shoulders.

"Enjoy yourself today?"

"Yes, thank you. Your boat is lovely. The company was great as well."

"My mother thinks you're special. In case you haven't noticed she's sort of a difficult lady."

"I think she's special."

Tre's thumb made circular patterns on her shoulders. His lips grazed her jawline. "I want to make love to you, baby. It's all I can think of. It's all that fills my head. I've wanted to do that from the very first time I'd laid eyes on you."

Caution. Proceed carefully. He was feeding her a line. What the hell, just don't take him too seriously and just go with the flow. She was a grown adult and there was nothing to stop her from having a fling. There might be consequences considering they lived right next door, but for tonight she was willing to live in the moment.

"You can pretty much have any woman you want," Jen countered. "You're considered a celebrity. Women are at your beck and call. Your apartment has a revolving door. Most leave there pretty unhappy. What's with that?"

"I'm not looking for a quick hit. Those days are over with. And quite frankly, I'm not crazy about being pursued."

His answer surprised her. She would have thought he'd eat up all the attention.

"What qualifies as not a quick hit?" she quizzed.

She'd just made it sound as if she was interrogating him. That should scare him off and send him running for home.

"I'm looking for a relationship," he came back with. "Full blown with all the romantic trimmings. I want to be with someone I have something in common with. She's got to be adventurous, flexible and secure. Just looking at her should make my mouth go dry."

"I would never have thought you were romantic."

"There's a lot you don't know about me."

"Amen."

Now he was rubbing her shoulders and leaning over to kiss her right on the lips. Jen was on sensory overload and digesting everything he'd just told her—the sight, manly smell and timbre of his voice literally made her toes curl. Soon she was clinging to him and kissing him back with a fierce passion that he'd aroused.

The hastily thrown-on wrapper was pooled at her feet. The balmy ocean breeze ruffled the T-shirt she'd worn to bed and cooled her heated cheeks. She was wired, every nerve ending alive.

Tre had the material of her shirt bunched in one hand. The other roamed her butt, cupping it slightly and squeezing. He'd pressed her hard against him and she could feel his growing erection.

Jen stood on tiptoe, kissing him back, delighting in the sensations his kiss evoked. She loved the feel and touch of him. The tingle that had started at her toes had worked its way up. Every nerve was alive and her center throbbed. Her breasts felt heavy, as if they would explode.

"Time to take this inside, baby," Tre suggested, putting her away from him.

Jen's breaths came in quick little bursts. She linked her fingers through Tre's and allowed him to lead her inside. Since their apartments basically had the same layout, he was up the hallway in a flash and inside her bedroom. Luckily she'd tidied up, just in case he followed through on his promise.

Tre was already kicking off his track pants. She tried not to stare at his strong muscular legs and the crisp dark hairs curling over them. When he unzipped the suit jacket, she caught a glimpse of a broad ebony chest and sculptured pectorals and a nest of dark hair.

Tre's smile warmed her. He took a long stride, closing the distance between them.

"You need help with that," he said, tugging the T-shirt over her head. When Jen stood in only her bikini panties, his hot gaze swept her body. He moistened a finger in his mouth and reached over to outline a nipple. She jumped.

Tre's other hand was already on her breast, kneading the soft flesh beneath his heated palm. She was already close to losing it. Her throbbing body wanted every inch of him. Jen put it down to being too long without a man; not that Anderson had been anything special in the sack, though he thought he was.

Tre stopped and was now rifling through the pocket of his discarded pants. He palmed an object and peeled off his underpants with his other hand, then he climbed under the covers.

"Join me, baby," he urged. "Let me love you."

"Shouldn't we talk about protection?"

"Taken care of." He opened his palm and showed her the gold foil package.

An experienced man. The alarm bells went off. Ignoring them, Jen slid under the covers. Tre's mouth immediately went to work loving her. His hands roamed all her moist places, delving into every crevice and then some. She was loving him back with her hands and mouth, laving him, and using her fingers to do her own intimate exploring.

His "Yes, baby, yes," gave her encouragement to be even more daring. They switched positions, alternating between pleasuring each other. Finally, Tre rolled her over on her chest and covered her body with his. Jen felt his coarse chest hairs graze her back as he ground into her. She felt his soft kisses on the sides of her neck and when he stopped to shield himself she felt abandoned. Then he was entering her with long, slow strokes which quickly built in intensity, and he was nibbling on her flesh and nipping her while making seductive heartfelt grunts.

Tre's ankles locked around hers. His hands slid under her body, one on her breast the other on her throbbing core. He'd filled her up and overwhelmed her with sensations. She was OD'ing on the sounds and smell of him, totally enjoying the feelings of wild abandonment and of going with the flow.

Jen hadn't expected Tre to be this tender or this giving. And she certainly did not expect to feel so uninhibited with a man that she had no relationship with to speak of, and probably would never have, once he found out she was *Dear Jenna*.

The first spasm sent her spiraling over the edge, and another one quickly followed. She could barely hold on or wait for him to come with her. He was right there as she slipped into that place where nothing else mattered except him and her. He was there with her, matching her gasp for gasp and taking her with him to the land of sensations.

"We are…good…together," he gasped.

"No, we're great."

She meant it. They complemented each other, the perfect sex mates.

At least for tonight.

Marva's eyes were on the bedside clock again. Midnight had come and gone and still no sign of Tre. One o'clock rolled around and he still hadn't returned. She wasn't worried.

Bless that boy, he'd snuck out when he thought she was asleep. She'd gotten a certain satisfaction from knowing he was heading for 5C's and she fully approved. Jen St. George was just what her restless son needed. The woman had a good head on her shoulders and wasn't one of those shallow bimbettes with nothing to say. She would settle Tre down.

Therefore Marva was even more delighted that her little ruse worked. Only a fool wouldn't notice Tre was crazy about that girl and she was crazy about him. It didn't take ESP to figure out what the two of them were up to. But both were consenting adults and any doubts about her son's sexuality had been put to rest.

She gave the clock another quick glance and decided to make good use of Tre's absence. Tre had lent her his laptop, supposedly to keep her entertained and out of his hair. He'd asked, no, ordered her to cancel his membership on Café Singles.

Marva booted up the computer and accessed the e-mail address she'd set up so candidates could reply to her ad. She scanned the e-mails just in case someone wonderful had replied. Much as she liked Jen, nothing in this world was guaranteed, and as her own mother used to say, every woman should have a backup man.

Personally she thought it was stupid of Tre not to give at least a look at some of the women who'd answered. The Internet provided a good way to screen out candidates and save both them and you a lot of heartache.

Marva was almost through reading the e-mails and scrutinizing the photos when the subject line of

one caught her eye. "Look Me Up For Advice," sure
was different. It was catchy. The girl had a sense of
humor.

But would the woman's wit match the accompanying photo? Marva knew her son well enough to
know that Tre liked his ladies well-groomed and
classy; at least she thought so, based on the two he'd
brought home. She downloaded the photo and waited
for the picture to pop up.

It was a professional picture and a little outdated.
She could swear she'd seen it before. No one wore
those pinstriped double-breasted suits these days
unless they were in banking; even the lawyers had
eased up. Now if the woman ditched the silly glasses
she wouldn't be half bad. It bothered her she couldn't
immediately place the face. She never ever forgot a
face. Maybe she was getting old.

"What are you doing, Mother?" Tre's voice came
out of nowhere.

One of Marva's hands immediately flew to her
chest, the other tried to log off quickly. Tre, in anti-
cipation of her move, had a firm hold on her wrist.

"Oh, no you don't." He scanned the screen and
looked at her with flashing eyes. Her boy had always
had a bad temper. Now she prayed she wouldn't be
on the receiving end. It usually surfaced when he

perceived an injustice was being done. Tre had since worked to rein in that temper, even taking anger management classes after he'd punched out a man for trying to steal an old lady's pocketbook. In the scuffle he'd actually broken the guy's nose.

"You told me you canceled this membership, Mother."

"I was going to."

Tre glanced at the monitor again and frowned. "What's this photo of Dear Jenna doing up? Tell me you're not meddling, Mother."

Suddenly it hit her. No wonder she knew that face. She'd seen it earlier, only a friendlier version. But the woman had been more casually attired so she'd come across as less stiff.

Marva looked at Tre. Poor sod. He didn't have a clue. Dear Jenna and Jen in 5C were one and the same. Jen had just sent him the message she was interested.

Should she leave the big doofus to figure it out himself? Or should she tell him? Men could be so dumb at times.

Chapter 18

"You get a response from that man we think is D'Dawg?" Chere huffed as she pedaled the stationary bike. They were at Flamingo Place's gym, seated on bikes next to each other.

Chere had asked Jen if she would let her use one of her visitor's passes. She claimed she wanted to look around as she was considering joining a gym. Something or someone had prompted her to put forth the effort because out of the blue she was making a concerted effort to work on her weight. What was up with that? It hadn't seemed to matter before. Chere always proudly referred to herself as having big beautiful curves. Her men seemed to like her that way.

"Haven't heard a word," Jen admitted, pedaling furiously. "You think his mama told him I responded?"

"Hard to say."

It bothered Jen that she had not heard word one from Tre ever since their passionate evening together. True, she had no hold on him. They didn't even have an understanding, but it was still troubling that she hadn't seen or heard from him. She'd already resolved it in her mind that if it was to be a onetime thing, at least she would have good memories.

"So why are you suddenly on this exercise kick?" she asked Chere after they switched to treadmills and Chere began a leisurely stroll on hers while Jen jogged.

"You inspire me," Chere said sincerely. "I want to get into one of those cute little outfits you wear out. I want to look like her." She pointed to the Latin woman, Jen recognized as the Pink Flamingo's hostess. She was using the stepper while talking to a man Jen thought might be the restaurant's manager. "I need to find me a professional man."

"How about a nice guy, just someone who treats you decently?"

"I'll settle for employed and one who's not paying his ex an arm and a leg in alimony or child support."

They high-fived each other and giggled.

"Well, it's nice to see you ladies making use of the facilities," a male voice said from in front of them.

Jen smiled brightly and waved at Quen Abraham the health-club manager. He looked especially fit outfitted in his black T-shirt and khaki shorts. He carried a clipboard under one arm.

"Hey, Quen, you know a good personal trainer?" Chere yelled.

Quen stopped and turned back. "As a matter of fact I know several. Is it for you?"

Chere nodded. She'd poured herself into Lycra capris and a sports bra she had no business wearing.

"Normally I don't do this, but I can make an exception. I'd work with you."

Chere shut off the machine and hurried over to make her negotiations. Several minutes later she returned looking pleased.

"Quen's letting me join the gym at the residents' price. He's also going to work with me three times a week."

"That's wonderful," Jen said warmly.

Later, showered and dressed, Jen retrieved the messages on her cell phone. One was from her boss, Luis. He wanted her to call the office immediately. Jen wondered what could be so urgent. Things had been relatively quiet now that the whole issue of "queer" had been resolved. She left Chere reading and cataloging and went into her bedroom to return the call.

Big mistake. The memories of her and Tre's lovemaking were still very fresh and, as much as she'd tried to put it all behind her, she had to admit she'd developed feelings for the man.

Now she concentrated on what Luis was saying. "I got a call from WARP's program director. He'd like to set up a radio debate between you and Doctor Love."

"You mean Doctor Allen Fraser."

"Exactly. *The Southern Tribune*'s raring to get you both on. They figure the PR will do them good, and I don't think it will hurt us, either."

"When is this debate supposed to be?"

"Primetime of course. Midweek, probably Wednesday, on the D'Dawg show."

Like she didn't have that one figured.

"We'll do this remotely like the last time. I'll call into WARP?" Jen asked.

"Well, actually no, the host wants you both to come down to the station."

That just couldn't happen. She needed to get out of this somehow.

"Why? That's so inconvenient."

"The program director mentioned something

about having you react to each other's comments face-to-face."

"I'd prefer to call in to the radio station," Jen insisted. "I'm already behind with two upcoming columns. This will set me back even more."

"You'll manage," Luis said, "You always do."

And that was that. Now her cover was in danger of being blown.

She disconnected and returned to the living area to find Chere still at her desk. So far she had not been sidetracked by Jen's kitchen or refrigerator. Chere was taking this business of getting into shape seriously. There had to be some particular reason. Jen strongly suspected it was because of a man.

Making a mental note to call the management office later, to let them know she might be interested in purchasing the apartment, Jen sat back down and involved herself in her work.

"Boris wants to see you," Bill said the moment Tre set down his bulging backpack holding the everpresent assortment of CDs.

Tre scrunched up his nose. "What does he want?"

"Who knows? I don't think he's on the warpath. He's actually been in a pretty good mood this evening."

Then it could be almost anything. Tre had shown up early at the radio station determined to have time to research his upcoming guests. He wanted to know more about this "love doctor," and what made him a specialist on relationships. He also meant to find out everything he could about *Dear Jenna*. No point in having an on-air debate unless you were prepared to ask some uncomfortable questions. This broadcast was going to rock.

Boris had his feet propped up on his desk when Tre entered. His hands were folded under his chin.

"Hey, you," he greeted.

"What's up?" Tre flopped down in the seat facing Boris and waited.

"I wanted you to be the first to know WARP will most likely be sold."

Tre was on his feet. "What? None of us had any warning of this."

"It was unexpected and an offer only a damn fool would refuse."

"What does this mean for me?" Tre asked.

"You're one of the lucky ones. You've got a great following and with the recent controversy, your ratings have gone right through the roof. You have nothing to worry about."

Tre inwardly heaved a sigh of relief, privately

thinking it was time to get word out on the street he
was looking for a job. New management often meant
uncomfortable changes. For the most part, he and
Boris got along; but who knew what these new
owners would be like?

Boris removed his feet from the console and stood
up, signaling the audience was over. "I'll be calling
a staff meeting shortly. Until then I would like you
to keep this under your hat."

"Sure thing," Tre said, turning away.

In the few minutes that the meeting had taken he'd
been given a lot to consider. He was smack in the
middle of negotiating buying his apartment and he'd
involved himself with his next-door neighbor whom
he'd not reached out to since that night. He needed a
little space and time to think.

He would put Jen out of his head and focus on the
impending radio interview with Miriam Young. He'd
worked hard to get the no-nonsense Flip-Flop
Momma on, and the day before the election at that.
This was one straightforward woman. She wasn't
about BS, she was about addressing issues and
righting wrongs.

Bill signaled. "Five minutes and you're on the air."

This gave Tre just a few seconds to scrutinize his
notes. He was off and running.

"Yo, Flamingo Beach. D'Dawg's on the air bringing you some of your favorite tunes this evening. We have live from our little downtown area, Miriam Young, who many of you think is your new mayor. Or was that Mayoress?" He paused, looking to Bill for help. "I'm told Mayor is politically correct, y'all. Anyway, this Flip-Flop Momma's not one to flip-flop on issues as the incumbent suggests. In half an hour or so we'll hear where this frank outspoken lady stands. And of course we're here to take your calls."

Tre pushed a button on the console and broke for commercials. Something felt off tonight. He attributed it to not knowing what to do about Jen.

But something clearly needed to be done before his mother took matters into her own hands.

Chapter 19

It was an odd hour of the morning for Jen's phone to ring. Most people would assume she was at work, not working out of the house. She was tempted to ignore it. Anyone Jen knew would reach her on her cell phone.

Today glancing at her caller ID wasn't helping, either. It flashed "blocked call." Totally useless. Still, something prompted Jen to answer.

"Hello."

"Bonjour, mademoiselle," the familiar voice said. "How is the most beautiful woman in the world?"

"Ellis!" Jen screamed. "It's been too long. Where are you?"

"Back in Paris. Jacques and I are simply exhausted. We trekked all over Spain and through Italy. Now we need a vacation after the vacation."

"I almost didn't answer," Jen admitted. "At this hour I'm usually bombarded with telemarketing calls, but I'm glad I did."

"Well, I'm glad you did, too," her brother answered, his delight at hearing her voice coming across the airwaves. "Jacques and I worry about you, especially after what that jerk did. He'll get his, I promise."

"Don't waste your energy on Anderson. I'm over him, fully recovered and moved on."

"Good. I never did like the sound of him. So there must be someone new, tell your little brother." Ellis must have picked up on something in her tone.

"Not exactly new," Jen said carefully. "We're exploring where we want to go with it."

"In other words, mind my business. Haven't I told you to move to Paris, the most romantic city in the world? The men here don't play games. They go after what they want. There's a substantial number of Algerians living here, not to mention the French men are crazy about African-American women."

It was an old conversation. Ellis the brother who'd had an even tougher time than she growing up, encouraging her to move to France where he felt comfortable and was fully accepted.

Ellis had been labeled the difficult child no foster family wanted. He and Jen had been split up more times than she cared to think about. What Ellis had been was confused about his sexuality and downright scared. They were two years apart and he'd loved playing with her dolls, grooming them meticulously and designing fashionable clothing for them to wear.

He'd been destined to be the successful designer he'd become. Ellis had been lucky to win a full scholarship to New York's Fashion Institute of Technology, where he majored in lingerie design. He'd met Jacques, an exchange student, their senior year, and had moved with him to Paris after they graduated.

"Actually I like it here," Jen admitted. "Flamingo Beach is quaint and charming. It's such a southern town. The architecture is beautiful. Most of the homes have these wonderful gardens."

"What about the people? How open-minded are they?"

Jen had to think about that carefully and the hubbub that had been caused over an unfortunate choice of words.

"Pretty conservative," she admitted.

"There, see? I rest my case. How about a visit then? I'll send you a ticket."

"I haven't been working for *The Chronicle* long enough to get vacation," she reminded Ellis.

"It would hardly kill them to give you a day off attached to a weekend. You mentioned in one of your many e-mails you spend some days working from home, so what does it matter whether you're in Florida or not? As long as you have a computer you can deliver."

So true, but she still needed time to think about it. They talked for a few more minutes, ending the call on an upbeat note that Jen would think about visiting for an extended weekend.

As usual she was left feeling connected and loved. Ellis made no bones about verbalizing how much he loved his big sister. Conversations like this one made her long for a family, a man she trusted, could confide in and feel safe with, even a couple of kids, a family unit.

Jen thought about the man next door who'd made no secret of wanting a relationship. But not with her she would guess. It had been several days since their passionate mating and nada since. Time to put an end to the cat-and-mouse game. She would knock on his door and reassure him it was perfectly okay with her. They could be friends. He needed to know she was a big girl and didn't have any expectations.

Besides, she wanted to see Marva again before she went home to Detroit. Tre's mother was unconventional and meddlesome but she had a huge heart. She only wanted what was best for her son.

He should be at home at this hour. He usually was. Feeling nervous and more flustered than she was willing to admit, Jen stood in front of 5B. She raised a hand, prepared to knock and then tucked it back into her pocket. She stood for a moment taking deep breaths and composing herself before raising her hand again. This time she managed a tentative knock. No answer. Should she try again? Was it worth it? She'd give it one last try. This time she folded her hand into a fist and gave a resounding rap.

"Just a minute," a female voice called.

She exhaled and tamped down on her disappointment, then reminded herself that because Marva had answered it didn't mean Tre wasn't home.

The door flew open. "Oh, child, it's so good to see you. I've been after that son of mine to try to set something up. Maybe a dinner or something, but you know how that goes. Men just aren't good at following through. Come in."

Marva stood aside to let Jen enter. "Are you alone?" she asked, looking around for signs of Tre.

"Yes, as a matter of fact I am. Tre had to run some errands then he was off to the gym."

"Do you have lunch plans?" Jen asked impulsively.

"My plans are with the refrigerator in there." Marva gestured toward the kitchen.

"Then let me take you to lunch."

"I'd love it."

"Just give me a few minutes to freshen up and I'll meet you in the lobby in fifteen minutes. Will that give you enough time?"

It seemed to work for Marva. Jen left her, glad that she'd taken the initiative to make contact again. For some strange reason it was important that Tre's mother liked her, she couldn't figure why.

At the appointed hour, Jen waited in the attractive lobby with its marble floors and mirrored walls. Pastel-colored sofas held plump pillows and were grouped around chrome-and-glass tables. The circular marble desk, behind which security presided, held two glass urns filled with calla lilies and ferns.

Marva came strolling out of the elevator wearing a wide-brimmed straw hat, matching purse and what was becoming her signature—another wild-print dress. Spotting Jen, she advanced.

"It's so nice to be getting out with someone other than Tre."

"I thought you were friends with Ida. At the reception the two of you seemed to be getting along quite well."

"We are, and we do, but it's still nice to be with someone young and energetic. So where are we going?"

"That depends on what you'd like to eat."

Marva thought about it as they walked outside. "To tell you the truth, I'm sick of seafood," she announced. "What I'd like is food that sticks to the gut. I'd like a good meat loaf, maybe a couple of pork chops and some juicy ribs."

"I know just the place," Jen said, linking an arm through Marva's. "It's not very fancy, though."

"I don't need fancy."

When they were in the Miata with the top down, Marva said, "So have you seen Tre recently?"

Jen was careful to school her face from having any reaction. "Not since our day in the sun. I guess he's been busy."

"His radio station's up for sale," Marva confided. "I think he's worried."

"Worried that he might not have a job?" Jen asked carefully.

"No, they assured him his job is safe. He's one of the more popular DJs around. His ratings have been phenomenal—at least that's what he tells me."

"So why is he worried then?"

"Well he's pretty much committed to buying his apartment, but now he's thinking this might be a good time to start looking around. You know, while he's hot. Tre has always dreamed of New York City. To him that would be the ultimate. It would mean he's arrived. He'd consider L.A. although it doesn't have the same cachet as New York, but it's got a huge urban population."

There was a knot in the pit of Jen's stomach as she pulled in to the parking lot of Tante Ann's.

"Let's find someone to seat us," she said, "then we can continue to talk."

They were led to one of the banquettes and handed a menu.

"Service is slow but the food is good," Jen warned.

"I don't have any place to be. Do you?"

"No." Just hundreds of letters needed to be answered. Chere, consumed by her new health-and-fitness kick, had started slacking off again.

They perused their menus, placed their orders and sat back to wait.

"Getting my lemonade sometime soon might be

nice," Marva muttered, looking around at the primarily African-American crowd.

"I warned you. So what do you think Tre will do?" she couldn't stop herself from asking.

Marva shrugged. "Hard to say. He's always been ambitious, unlike my other son, constantly in and out of trouble with the law. That child left home at sixteen and never returned, which is just fine with me. Let him be somebody else's problem."

Jen had no idea Tre even had a brother. Now she realized she knew very little about him.

"What about Tre's father?" she asked.

"What about him? He's not around if that's what you're asking. He's never really been around. We were married only long enough to have two children, then he took off."

Their lemonades finally arrived.

"Thank you, Jesus," Marva said to the waitress. "I could have dropped dead of thirst."

"And you raised two children single-handedly," Jen continued after the young woman had left.

"As best as I could."

"You're to be admired."

"I did what any mother would do."

And finally the food arrived. So far still no mention of the e-mail or photo she'd sent. Marva had to have recognized her. She obviously read the *Dear Jenna* column unless she'd thought it was a joke. Maybe she'd thought someone was goofing with her and had scanned the photo right from the newspaper. There was always that possibility.

Marva ate her pork chops, greens and mashed potatoes with relish, then set her knife and fork aside. She ordered the sweet-potato pie, then told the waitress she hoped it wouldn't take as long as the main course did.

Turning her attention to Jen, she said, "So what are you going to do about my son?"

The question blindsided Jen.

"Sorry, I don't understand."

"You do, too. Don't give me that."

Marva folded her arms over her ample bosom and waited.

"Tre and I really don't know each other that well," Jen stammered. "We're pretty much just next-door neighbors."

"I've seen you two together. It doesn't appear that way to me."

Curious to hear what Marva thought, Jen asked, "What were your impressions?"

"What I saw was a lot of tenderness. I saw two people very interested in each other but afraid to

make the first move. That boy had me worried for a
moment, if you know what I mean. He was showing
no signs of settling down. He had taken to wearing
these hip outfits and that diamond stud in his ear.
Well, that bothered me."

Jen felt a compelling need to come to Tre's
defense. "He's a radio personality. He has an image
to maintain."

"As long as it's just an image. Anyway, the two of
you need to work out your situation and get on with
it. Whatever it is. You've got my blessing."

"I don't think Tre is that interested in me," Jen
admitted, not adding that he hadn't called her or tried
to make contact since that night.

"I think you're wrong. The mistake most of you
young women make is that you still wait for the man
to declare himself and that's just not going to happen.
We're dealing with the fragile male ego here." She
held a hand up. "Now I'm not suggesting you get
pushy or anything but the secret is to make them
think it's their idea. Plant a seed in their heads and
let them take it from there. But you know that."
Marva sat back looking at her.

Was that a shot? It certainly sounded like the type
of advice she'd give someone who had written to her.
But there was still that matter of Tre not knowing who

she was and his reaction when he found out. He might very well feel deceived and decide he wanted nothing to do with her.

But he hadn't initially told her who he was, either. She'd found that out by other means, although his reasons for omitting mentioning who he was, were different than hers. He hadn't intentionally set out to deceive her the way that she had set out to deceive him. He'd just wanted to make sure that it was he she was really interested in and not the radio persona.

Marva's eyes sparkled but her tone was deadly serious. "Put your *Dear Jenna* hat on and follow her advice."

They smiled at each other.

Chapter 20

The ballots had all supposedly been counted and the Flip-Flop Momma had lost. The majority of Flamingo Beach's residents were fired up and accusations were being hurled. A recount was being demanded. There was talk of stuffed ballot boxes and dysfunctional voting equipment as well as voters being turned away and told they were ineligible.

WARP was flooded with phone calls. It was all that most people seemed to want to talk about. Tension could be felt in the streets and there was even talk of rioting. All of a sudden the sleepy little haven had come alive and emotions were running high.

Tre of course took advantage of this. It kept his program popping and an audience glued to the radio. Now people didn't seem all that interested in hearing from *Dear Jenna* and Doctor Love. He suggested to the program director that they move the debate to another week and he agreed.

Meanwhile Marva's two weeks were close to coming to an end but she showed no signs of wanting to go home. He wasn't sure what to do about that, either. And he still wasn't sure what he wanted to do about Jen. He'd already let it drag out way too long. Going for a long tiring run might very well help clear his head. Then he could decide how to proceed.

Tre had just returned from a five-mile run. Breathless and weary, he limped to the apartment. His mother greeted him with the wave of a thick courier package.

"Can you take this next door?" she asked. "I signed for it because there was no one at home."

She'd been in the apartment practically all day. Enough time to ensure the package was reunited with its owner.

"Set it down on the table. Whose is it anyway, Camille Lewis's, Ida's? I'll grab a quick shower and I'll run it over, then we can decide what we're doing for dinner."

Marva didn't respond, which was unusual for her.

Freshly showered and dressed, Tre returned to the living room to find his mother leafing through some real-estate pamphlets she must have picked up on one of her walks.

"Are you thinking of buying property here in North Florida, Mother?" he joked.

"As a matter of fact I am."

Oh, lord, his world was closing in around him. "So that means you would consider selling the house in Detroit?" The house he had cosigned on and helped her buy.

"I like Florida living," Marva admitted.

"I may not be in Florida very long," Tre warned.

"That's okay. I make friends easily. Look at the friends I've already made here. Besides if you leave you'll need someone to watch over your apartment. You are still planning on buying it?"

Over his dead body was he going to leave his mother unsupervised in Flamingo Place stirring up all kinds of trouble. "I'm too far in the process to back out now," he replied.

She shook the envelope at him. "Don't forget this needs to be delivered."

"Okay, I'll take it. Where to?"

Marva smiled gleefully. "It's Jen's in 5C. I will presume you know your way over."

Tre glared at her. Why did he feel this was some sort of setup or he was being conspired against? He might as well get it over with. He needed to talk to Jen anyway. Tre accepted the envelope, tucking it under his arm.

"I'll only be gone a few minutes," he said. "By the time I get back you should be ready to go."

"We'll see."

Tre felt himself tense up as he stood before Jen's door. He'd allowed almost a week to go by and he wondered how she would react upon seeing him again. He on the other hand was looking forward to seeing her now that he had a clearer head. He'd thought things through and realized there was no reason to panic. He did not have a stalker on his hands or a weepy woman, calling him a hundred times a day to determine what happened.

They were both adults. He could admit he liked her, more than liked her. But she'd made it clear that she wasn't necessarily looking to get involved and there lay the problem. He'd tried to convey he was over casual flings and recreational sex. They served no useful purpose that he could see. He needed to start thinking about having a family, regardless of whether Florida continued to be home.

Sucking in a breath, Tre pressed the buzzer. He balanced the courier-delivered package on his open palm. Something made him take a look at the address label. Why was Jen getting a delivery from *The Flamingo Beach Chronicle?* He examined the address closely. Yes, the package was meant for Jen St. George but why did it say, *Re: Dear Jenna?*

He didn't like the thoughts that were beginning to formulate in his head. Impossible! She couldn't be. But then again, it made sense. It would explain her evasiveness when he'd tried to pin her down about her career. It would explain her presence at those high-profile affairs, and it would even explain the T-shirt she'd given his mother.

And she'd made a fool of him. A red-hot anger flooded him; anger that he'd worked all his life to control. To think he was just starting to care for the woman. He was tempted to drop the box in front of her door and simply leave. No wonder she didn't need a man. She had a decent job giving advice to trusting fools. She was the one who'd coached his mother and encouraged her to follow up and place some stupid personal ad on the Internet. Just the thought of it made him more enraged.

The door of 5C slowly opened up. "Tre," Jen said, her smile warm and welcoming. "What a nice surprise. Come on in."

Grim-faced he entered and handed over the package. "This arrived today. My mother signed for it."

Jen accepted the box, barely glancing at it. "Please thank Marva for me. How are you? I was beginning to think you moved," she joked.

"I'm doing quite well, thank you."

He was over the small talk already, sick to death of it. How could this woman he'd made love to like there was no tomorrow stand there with her eyes sparkling, pretending that she was glad to see him?

"Aren't you going to open your package, Jenna?" He made sure to enunciate the name. Tre waited for the expected reaction. She did not disappoint him.

As what he'd just said sank in there was a visible reaction, a slight jerking of the head, a quick blinking of the eyes, then she composed herself.

"You know?" she said. "How long have you known?"

"You might want to check the name on the label of that package."

"Oh, I see."

"Is that all you have to say?"

He refused to let those innocent hazel eyes distract him. He was over being conned. And even though she was standing there looking lovely, and vulnerable, he just wasn't going to be taken in again.

When the silence dragged on Tre felt compelled to say something.

"To think I let you play me. This was all a game for you. The whole thing, befriending my mother, pretending you had an interest in me…sleeping—"

"Hold it…"

But he was not about to hold it. His temper erupted. He let loose on her with both barrels.

"You're supposed to be an advice columnist, able to read people, an expert on human dynamics. Where's your sensitivity? Do you have integrity or ethics? You spout the rhetoric, but when it comes time to walk the walk you're just not capable."

"If you'd allow me to explain—"

"What's there to explain? You were trying to prove something to yourself. You used me. You used my mother."

"I did not."

Then he remembered the photo his mother had been trying to hide on the Internet, and his fury spiraled out of control.

"You're pretty damn shameless," he shouted, totally losing it now. "You'd stoop so low as to sleep with me so that you could prove to my mother that your advice works. Anything for that damn column of yours!"

"That's just not true," Jen shouted back.

He needed to regain control of himself. Take a few deep breaths and cool down. All those months of classes working on his temper were rapidly going out the window.

"Then why do it to begin with?" he shouted. "What were you trying to prove, that you could seduce me?"

"Who seduced whom?" she screamed. "You showed up at my door and the idiot that I am, I let you in."

"Puh-lease. You wanted to make love as much as I did. I told you I would be by later to finish what I started. So let's not pretend it wasn't consensual."

A splash of something ice-cold hit him in the face. Tre swiped away at the drops. He hadn't seen that coming. Where had she gotten that glass from?

"Why you little—" He advanced on her, prepared to remove the water from her hand should the need arise. A loud banging on the front door stopped him midstep.

"Security!"

Jen looked at him. He looked at her.

This time the rapping was louder and more insistent.

"Security, Ms. St. George, are you okay? We've had a report of a loud disturbance."

Jen's fingers now worried her forehead. She'd simmered down a bit. "Just what I need."

"Just what we both need. Better answer the door before someone calls the cops."

"I'll be right there," Jen called and went off to answer.

By the time she'd opened the door Tre had calmed down considerably. Two young bright-eyed security types, neither of whom he recognized, stood on the threshold taking in the scene.

"Is there a problem?" one of them asked.

"No problem," Jen said flashing a smile. "Was my stereo too loud or something?"

"Actually no, ma'am. We had a report of a loud disturbance coming from your apartment."

The shorter of the guards squinted at him. "D'Dawg, is that you, man? I heard you lived in one of these fancy cribs. I couldn't believe my luck getting this job."

No point in pretending that he was not who he was. He nodded at the awed guard. "I think there may have been a misunderstanding. As you can see, there's no issue here. I'm sorry you were bothered," he quickly said.

"No problem. Just as long as everything's all right now."

Camille Lewis chose that moment to stroll by. She made a point of stopping at the open door.

"Was there a break-in or something?" The question was directed to the guards. When they didn't respond right off she seized the opportunity to stick her head inside Jen's apartment. "Oh, Tre is that you?" she cooed. "You must have stopped by to fix the plumbing."

What a bitch.

Tre chose to let it go. He'd already allowed himself to be baited once tonight and he'd almost returned to a place he'd promised himself never to go.

"Thank you, gentlemen," Jen said with some finality. "I'm sorry you were inconvenienced." She closed the door on them and turned back to him.

"Satisfied? Feeling better you got all that anger off your chest? Think we can talk?"

He nodded slowly.

Tre didn't know about talking. What he was willing to do was listen. Listen and hope her explanation was one he could buy.

Chapter 21

"This was never really about you," Jen said, ending her monologue almost half an hour later. "I didn't know your identity at the time, so trust me, I had no axe to grind."

Tre had listened intently to her explanation, never once interrupting. She'd even admitted to him that she'd dispensed her advise to Ms. Mabel, aka Marva, not expecting her to really take it. She'd also admitted her reticence in letting not just Tre, but anyone know that she was the illustrious *Dear Jenna*. Anonymity was key in a business more often than not grossly misunderstood.

And she'd shared with him that once they'd gotten over their neighborly misunderstanding, and become friends, she didn't think he would have cared who she was.

Tre did break his silence once to ask, "So why go to the lengths of responding to this ridiculous ad Mother posted if you didn't intend to stick it to me?"

"You're wrong," she'd insisted. "Your mother and I connected. We got along from the beginning. The message I was sending to the screener of your e-mails, and matchmaker extraordinaire, is that I'm interested. I figured Marva would find a way to let you know."

It was a brave confession. Jen had bared her soul. She'd been as honest as she could be with him. And even after that soul-baring confession, he'd said he needed time to think. That was the last she'd heard or seen of him. Jen had already resigned herself to thinking that they were over with. She questioned if they'd actually ever gotten started. Ironic, that she, the silver-tongued advice columnist, quick on the draw with the advice, had botched things up this badly.

And as usual, to take her mind off things, she focused on her work for the next few days. Work and negotiating the purchase of an apartment in the building, except not the one she currently lived in. A beautiful two-bedroom on a higher floor was still up for sale. The property owner was asking a little more than she'd hoped to spend, but all things considered, it was a steal for waterfront.

Marva had gone home, she presumed. She hadn't heard a word from her and that was a little disappointing. She'd assumed they were friends. The show in which she and Doctor Love were supposed to share air space never happened and Jen assumed that was Tre's doing, as very clearly he wanted nothing to do with her.

Chere, who was miraculously sticking to her diet and exercise routine, told her she was being ridiculous. She'd even mentioned there had been reruns of the D'Dawg show for the last week or so. This had made Jen think Tre might be out of town. Maybe he'd taken his mother home.

Jen still couldn't bring herself to admit she missed Tre's presence, and the excitement of having him right next door. What she did admit was that she felt lethargic and strangely out of step. Almost overnight Flamingo Beach had lost a lot of its charm. And she actually felt lonely and homesick.

And so on a Tuesday night, with little else to do, Jen had headed for the only gourmet grocery store in town catering to the health-and-fitness crowd. She was surprised to run into Eileen Brown in the produce section.

"Hey, girl," Eileen said as they moved off to the side allowing other shoppers to go by. "We never seem to have the time to do lunch these days. Are you in a hurry, or do you have time for coffee?"

"I'm heading home to more work," Jen answered. "I'd love to have coffee with you and catch up."

Eileen led the way to the little café smack in the middle of the store that sold exotic coffees and frothy lattes. They grabbed cappuccinos. Jen just couldn't resist adding a macadamia-and-white-chocolate-chip cookie to her tray, justifying it with, "I deserve this."

They found seats on high stools next to the railing seeparating the café from the grocery store.

"So what do you think about this whole fiasco with the mayoral election?" Eileen asked.

Jen rolled her eyes. "Personally I think it's an embarrassment. Other states don't seem to have a problem getting their voting right. Mention Florida and we're the butt of every bad joke."

"So true. There's been recount after recount. An independent auditor was brought in, and Solomon Rabinowitz was still declared the winner. We need to move on."

"I agree."

Eileen took a sip of her drink and asked carefully, "Are you getting out much?"

"What's that supposed to mean?"

"Dating?"

A sore topic as far as she was concerned. She'd sworn off men even before meeting Tre. Now she was even more determined not to go there. She had enough to do. Work and acquiring the apartment should be enough to fill her life. The stab of betrayal, her feelings of hurt were still too new to discuss with anyone.

"I had an inquiry about you. Actually Barry did."

"You did?" Jen asked because it seemed the polite thing to do. She was more interested in the cappuccino in front of her than the person inquiring about her.

"Some guy called Vince. He's a contractor of sorts. He and Barry have done some work together in the past. He may have seen us together at the African-American Library. Naturally he was interested in the new girl in town."

"I'm hardly new anymore." Jen took a sip of the foaming liquid. "Mmmmm, good. I may have met him at the Pink Flamingo. He was the guy who bought me a drink."

"He's really not a bad sort. Divorced, has a little girl. Pretty much hardworking."

She felt compelled to put a stop to any fanciful notions Eileen might have. "I'm not interested."

"That sounds so final."

"It is."

Eileen decided to let it go at that.

"Guess who I heard was offered a job in New York?"

Jen sat back prepared to listen, thinking it was probably someone from *The Tribune*. She made a feeble attempt to guess.

"No, wrong on all counts. It's no one from the paper. It's your boy, Tre Monroe. He's hit the big time."

Just the sound of Tre's name made so many memories return. She even missed his loud music.

"Where did you find that out?" Jen asked.

"I have my ways. There's talk of it in a couple of New York papers. It's a Long Island radio station that's made the offer. Not exactly New York City but close enough. Supposedly he's been going back and forth, negotiating the deal. I don't think things are finalized yet."

"He's supposed to be in the midst of purchasing his apartment," Jen said out loud. "I wonder how that's all going to work out."

Warming to her subject, Eileen leaned in. "Usually if somebody wants you badly they'll make it worth your while. It would be nothing for a major station to turn around and buy that apartment from him and then flip it. He wouldn't lose a dime. Waterfront properties hold their value. But you know that. I'm preaching to the choir."

"Well, I'm happy for him if that's what he wants. I doubt WARP will be the same without the D'Dawg show though."

"I'm surprised you'd say that," Eileen said, shooting Jen a questioning look. "Especially considering all the trouble he caused you."

"Well, it worked to both of our advantages, didn't it. His ratings soared and he became sought-after. I secured myself a solid readership. And if I'm smart I need to cash in on it and see if I can squeeze another nickel or two out of Luis."

"Squeeze being the operative word."

They both chuckled. The conversation took a different turn.

"What are you doing for Memorial weekend?" Eileen asked.

"I'm toying with the idea of going to Paris."

"Ooh, la la! You've come into some bucks." Eileen's French manicured nails beat a gentle rhythm against the Formica table. "Or is there a more romantic reason for your considering heading for the City of Lights?"

"My brother lives there. He's invited me and he's willing to pay for the ticket."

"Then it's a no-brainer. Girl, I'd be on that plane in a New York minute." She snapped her fingers, making her point.

Maybe she should get on a plane and wing her way to Europe. A few days in Paris might help straighten out her head and give her a different perspective on things. Besides, it had been at least two years since she'd seen her brother Ellis and his partner Jacques. They would treat her like a queen and pamper her to death. Drowning herself in work just wasn't doing it for her anymore. Jen was slowly coming to the realization there had to be more to life than work.

Tre had gotten right off the flight from New York and headed to the radio station. It had been a great trip and he should have been feeling elated and on top of the world. His final interview with WLIR had gone much better than he'd anticipated. The station management had actually agreed to almost all of his demands, several of which bordered on the outrageous.

Tre's goal had been to infiltrate the tough New York market. He'd wanted to draw the hip urban types from the city and surrounding boroughs; people who were street-smart and on the cutting edge, and not easily offended. He wanted to be "the next great black hope" for young boys coming up with no particular career aspirations.

And sure he might be settling, but an offer from a radio station on Long Island wasn't something you turned up your nose at. His audience would be mostly from the 'burbs, and the demographics would be a bit different.

On the other hand, broadcasting from the tip of Long Island offered a challenge, and one he felt fully able to step up to. If he could reach a stiff conservative audience like Flamingo Beach, then the more worldly types on Long Island should be a snap.

He'd asked, no, demanded actually, a salary almost double what he was making, plus housing for at least six months until he was settled. He'd also explained that he was in the middle of purchasing a home and something would need to be worked out.

The management of WLIR didn't blink an eye when he'd presented his long list. He'd been assured most of his demands would be met. Next week he'd be receiving a formal offer to come aboard WLIR.

Tre should have been excited at the prospect but for some peculiar reason he was not. As he sat there minutes before his broadcast was to begin, his mind ran to Jen. He'd thought about her often and wondered what this might mean for them if he accepted the job.

He'd made no secret of it that he was job-hunting and had even told Boris that. To date, the new management of WARP had not made themselves known, nor had they so much as called a staff meeting. A smart man needed to look out for himself.

Minutes before the broadcast went live, Bill wandered in. He looked grim and was slugging water from the bottle in his hand. He handed Tre a memo.

Without so much as glancing at the piece of paper, Tre said, "What is this, Bill?"

"Maybe you should read it after the show."

"That bad?"

"Not good."

He glanced at the paper noting an emergency meeting was being called tomorrow during the day. It was mandatory for all station personnel to attend.

"Great!"

"And another thing," Bill said, before turning away. "We have that cruise ship drawing to do tonight. There's hundreds of entries, everything from business cards to jottings on napkins."

Tre sighed heavily. "What time is this drawing supposed to occur?"

"Right after your interview with Reverend Hal."

The Reverend Hal Bemis was a controversial guy; a self-appointed defender of the people. He spent a great deal of time stirring poor black folks up and igniting them to action, merited or not.

Bill's two fingers were now in the air. "Two minutes to broadcast."

Tre did his thing, rolling easily into his D'Dawg persona and loving every moment of it. He played his tunes, took a jab or two at the reverend, and took some calls. Tonight's audience seemed a bit different from the norm. He was used to them being feisty and outspoken but tonight's crowd seemed not only belligerent, but bitter. He'd never seen so much hatred and anger spewed. Several times he was forced to cut off one or another. At other times he was just grateful that there was a delay button.

"Man, I'm actually looking forward to doing something positive like announcing the winner of that cruise," he said to Bill during a commercial break.

"I hear you."

Things went downhill from there. Reverend Hal was on his soapbox about the recent election. According to him it was time that an African-American was at the helm. He seemed to have forgotten that no candidate of color had come forward to date. Then it was on to the price of real estate in the area. This he viewed as a conspiracy to drive black folks out.

By the time Tre opened the lines for questions he had an enormous headache. Reverend Hal was not the type of guest you could reel in. His followers were for the most part as bitter and angry as he, and the few callers who made sense were quickly shut down by the other respondents.

At last the show was almost over with and Bill was there with a sealed envelope holding the name of the cruise winner.

"And on a final uplifting note," Tre announced, "we got a winner for that Fun-Ship Cruise for two. Drumroll, please."

The sound effects kicked in, ending just as he held the business card in his hand.

It took pretty much every bit of professionalism Tre had left to make that announcement.

"Our winner is, Jen St. George from right here in Flamingo Beach. Believe it or not, folks, she's my next-door neightbor." And because he could no longer go on, Tre broke for music.

Chapter 22

Ellis and Jacques's pied-à-terre was located on the left bank of Paris in walking distance of the Eiffel Tower. It was a beautifully appointed place just as Jen expected it to be.

Jacques was an interior designer whose unique personality found expression in the decor. The whole effect was like being in a Middle Eastern bazaar. Every time Jen looked around there was some unusual piece of art, craft or tapestry to admire.

On Jen's second evening in Paris Ellis and Jacques had decided to have friends over. Huge hemp mats were arranged on the mosaic tile floors and colorful tableware set down. Tasseled toss cushions took the place of stiff chairs and added to the comfortable, casual atmosphere.

Jacques and Ellis's friends were an eclectic mix of people and weren't necessarily limited to the world of fashion. Invited was the married English couple, Bernard and his wife Stephanie, who'd taken a trip to Paris one summer and had never gone home. There was Miguel and Ven who were partners. One was Spanish and the other Vietnamese, and there was a lovely Swedish model Elsa who'd come on her own. As had the handsome Algerian, Jean Pierre, who Ellis had whispered into her ear was fabulously rich and knew how to please his ladies.

Dinner was eaten leisurely with several bottles of wine poured. As the evening progressed it seemed as if more and more people spilled from the apartment and into the tiny hallway. Even the little rooftop garden was packed. Snippets of conversations spoken in virtually every language floated Jen's way.

She stood on the rooftop feeling amazingly content while looking out on the lights of the city thinking of how Ellis had surely come into his own. The whole scene was so him. She, on the other hand, liked things a little quieter. Not that she was complaining. She'd been glad to get away, grateful to go to a place where no one expected much from her

other than her presence. At Ellis's, love was uncon-
ditionally given.

An arm slipped around her waist. "You've been
missed, hon," Ellis said into her ear. "Several of our
straight male friends have inquired about you. Jean
Pierre seems especially taken."

"Oh, you're just trying to make me feel better," Jen
said, covering his hand around her waist with her own.

"No, I'm not. You're easily the most attractive
woman I invited, especially since I convinced you to
splurge on that haircut." He playfully patted the new
brush cut with the attractive burgundy highlights Jen
sported. "So why so sad?"

"Does it show?"

They'd been trying to get some time alone since
she'd arrived but it hadn't happened until now.

"Oh, yes, big-time. Must be a man. Now don't
deny it."

Ellis was amazingly astute. He always had been.
He tilted her chin upward. "So what's his name?"

"Tre."

"*Very Tres,*" Ellis said, grimacing at his own
feeble joke.

"Trestin's his real name."

"And what does he do?"

She hesitated, already knowing what Ellis's reaction would be. "He's a radio personality."

"You mean disk-jockey type?" Ellis said, and began to giggle. Then, noting Jen's stricken expression, he said, "Sorry, hon. I'll try to contain myself."

"It's a perfectly respectable profession," she said as his mirth again threatened to explode.

"Who said it wasn't? It's just you, the diva of love, the preacher of stability and a disk jockey. I just can't see it."

She found herself defending the man who she still wasn't sure how she felt about. "Tre is perfectly respectable. He owns a car, and a boat and is in the process of purchasing his apartment and even has a mother I've met."

"You met his mother? Things must be serious then. No man introduces you to his mother unless he feels there's some potential there."

She supposed what Ellis said was true and she'd botched it big-time. She should never have acted impetuously and shot off that e-mail and photo in reply to that ad on Café Singles. That more than anything else had pissed Tre off.

"So what are you going to do about this man of yours?" Ellis asked, rubbing his cheek against hers.

"Nothing. There's nothing to do. He may be moving to New York anyway from what I've heard."

Ellis grasped her chin with his free hand, forcing Jen to look at him. "Hon, you're being an idiot. You're the one in control here. I don't know what happened between the two of you, but if you let that man go without at least telling him how you feel about him… well…well, I'll be disappointed. What would you tell a reader who wrote in with your problem?"

"To take the initiative if it meant that much. To get the situation resolved one way or the other. That she was doing it for herself and not necessarily him."

"Beautiful, *bébé.*" Ellis chucked her under her chin. "That's my girl. It's all about you. Now let's go back inside and see what Jacques is up to. And you, my darling, can flirt with Jean Pierre all you like but take it no further. He is—as they say—married."

Feeling as if a load had been taken off her chest, Jen kept an arm around her brother's waist and walked back into the apartment with him.

"You got it going on, girl!" Chere screamed, the moment she spotted Jen's new haircut. "You get that in Paris?" She fingered the material of the sleeveless linen dress that Jen wore with a shrug to pull it together and because she was going into the office today.

Her screams drew the attention of other members of the news team who'd arrived at the office early.

"Great hair on you," one of the secretaries shouted from over the top of her cubicle.

"I want that dress," another person in passing said.

The compliments served to make Jen feel like a million bucks. Altogether she'd had a great weekend. Outstanding really. She'd sorted through all the things that had weighed heavily on her mind and she'd returned determined to resolve them.

"You look great," she said to Chere, meaning it. "You had to have lost so far at least ten pounds."

"Mmm-hmm."

Her assistant had at least a hundred and fifty more to go but you had to start somewhere.

Jen eyed her in-box, surprised to find it almost empty. Chere had actually been doing some work in her absence and on a holiday weekend at that. Miracle of miracles.

"I brought you something," Jen said, dipping into the paper bag she carried. The gift had been purchased on a whim and as an inspiration to Chere.

Jen handed the exquisitely wrapped box over, then dug back into the paper bag to remove the truffles and coffee beans she'd brought for the staff.

Meanwhile, Chere's long nails plucked away at the pink-and-lavender ribbon the package was secured by. She flipped open the box.

"Oh, my, God!" she shrieked as she recognized what the gift was. Hooking the thong bikini bottom over one finger she waved it around and around. "I'm going to need to try these on."

Her high-pitched shrieks naturally drew the staff's attention again. Chere proudly paraded the itsy-bitsy French bikini around. Jen's present had apparently made her very happy.

Jen settled in. She'd come to work early with the express purpose of getting organized before the day officially began. It had only been a three-day weekend, four for her since she'd taken an additional day off, but even so there seemed an unusually high number of voice-mail messages. She'd attack those first.

For the most part they were the usual, people who'd bypassed the screening process and were hoping to get an audience with Jenna. Eileen had called not realizing she was out. She'd wanted to set up a day and time for lunch. There'd been a couple of other calls from staff members with one inquiry or another and there were several from WARP asking her to call.

Jen actually felt her breathing quicken. Could any of the half-dozen messages that were left be from Tre? Then she remembered the debate that never happened. That was most likely what those messages were about. She'd return the calls when she got around to it. She had much too much catching up to do today to make a return phone call a high priority.

And so it was later that afternoon, when the phone rang, she delegated its answering to Chere as she'd done all day.

"Diva Advice," Chere sang, making up the title and simultaneously making herself sound important.

Jen shot her a look.

"Oh, my God, oh, my God!" She stomped a heavy platform-shod foot then rocked back and forth. "I have to sit down."

Jen looked up from her typing, concerned. "What is it? What's the matter?"

"You gotta be kidding me!"

Chere was practically wheezing. Concerned that her admin was having some kind of attack, Jen bolted out of her seat, bringing her own bottled water with her.

"Breathe," she admonished.

And she was. Chere, while still clinging to the receiver, was breathing heavily through her mouth.

Jen attempted to get her to relinquish the equipment and finally settled for pressing her ear to the receiver.

"This is Jen St. George, are you still there?"

Canned music came at her, then loud applause. A man's deep voice boomed, "You're a winner, Jen St. George. You've won our Fun Ship Cruise for two."

"Okay, what are you trying to sell?"

"We're not trying to sell you anything. You're our winner."

"I didn't enter any contest."

"Perhaps you forgot. In any case your business card was selected from amongst a record number of entries."

Still huffing and puffing, Chere pointed to herself. It took Jen a while to get it. She covered the mouth of the receiver and angled an ear at her.

"Remember that Ford dealership opening?"

"Yes?"

"WARP had a booth that was off the chain. I had several of your business cards on me. You know I carry them in case you forget…."

"You entered me in this contest?"

"I entered us several times. It was just another way to help get us on that cruise ship."

Relinquishing the receiver to Jen she pretended to lead her own conga line.

"I'm feeling hot, hot, hot!"

Not! Not! Not! Jen thought. Definitely not!

Chapter 23

Tre sat in the chair the new owners of WARP had waved him into and waited for them to start the meeting. He should have felt anxious but he didn't. He'd been preparing himself for this all along, and he had a backup plan, an ace card to pull out of his pocket if need be. He'd come prepared to listen to what the brothers had to say.

For the past week his colleagues at the station had been grumbling and overall morale had been low. This had been especially noticeable after the mandatory staff meeting where the two brothers had announced they were taking over. Had they tried talking to the staff, things might have been very different. No one liked being dictated to and read a list of changes and policies. Even worse was not being allowed to ask questions.

During the week some of the staff had mysteriously disappeared. Speculation of course had run rampant. It was believed they'd been fired or simply jumped ship. Tensions were now at an all-time high, and attitudes were expressed in ways that were not necessarily beneficial to the radio station.

Supposedly there was to be a gradual transition of ownership. But with no official communication, people were running scared and team spirit had virtually disappeared.

"We've been meaning to get together with you before now," Zachary, the oldest of the two brothers said, resting his butt on the edge of the desk.

Tre said nothing.

Joshua, the shorter of the two, cleared his throat. "We wanted you to know how much you're valued at the station. Your ratings are by far the highest of any on-air personality."

"I'm aware of that," Tre said, wishing they would cut to the chase.

"Keep doing what you're currently doing and you'll have a job for life."

Tre nodded, guessing this was their reassurance talk.

"You must have questions." This came from Zach.

"I have several."

Tre listed them and waited as the brothers spewed their rhetoric. They weren't bad men, but it was clear they didn't have much experience in the business. Tre had worked for one owner previously who didn't have a clue.

He'd come aboard thinking that radio was a glamorous business. What he'd found out was that the hours were unpredictable, the politics awful and the turnover high. Radio, like any other revenue-generating business, relied on ratings and ratings assured sales. The two invariably went hand in hand.

The brothers were now droning on. Tre had heard enough to figure out how to play this. He stood.

"Well, I certainly appreciate your faith in me, but it needs to be backed up with something more substantial like a contract and dollars. What I'm saying is I would like some security."

Both brothers exchanged looks. They had to have seen what was coming.

"Well, we would be willing to talk about an attractive package," Zach hedged. "Give us a few days to put it together.

It was time to play his ace card. "I should tell you I have another offer."

Bonzo and Bozo actually gaped. Josh sputtered, "But we thought you were happy at WARP. At least that's what your predecessor led us to believe."

Tre studied his fingernails. Let them worry. "I'm not unhappy at WARP," he said after a while. "Management has been very good to me. I have a prime-time slot but the broadcast needs to be taken to the next level. I've been offered my own syndicated show along with the money to go with it. I would expect WARP to match both of those offers."

"Can we ask what salary you negotiated?" The question came from Joshua.

Tre named the figure.

Neither blinked an eye.

"There's also that contract that we'd need to talk about," Tre reminded them.

"We'll get back with you shortly." Zach squeezed his shoulder. "Don't worry. It'll all be good."

"I'll need an answer by tomorrow so that I can make my decision."

"You'll have one."

He left both brothers looking as if they'd just been run over by a sixteen-wheeler.

Jen set the mail on the dining room table as she always did before slowly going through the stack. She'd only been gone four days, yet judging by the bills and junk mail you wouldn't think so. She picked up the one personal-looking piece of correspondence amongst the bunch. It had no return address.

Curious as to the contents, she slid a nail under the

flap of the envelope and removed a card. Three African-American women of varying ages dressed in colorful kente-cloth dresses danced across the border. Jen's lips curved into a smile as she scanned the signature. Then she read the accompanying note.

Tre's mother wrote just like she spoke, using very few commas. She wanted Jen to know she'd made it back to Detroit safely, and was now signed up for line dancing classes with her neighbor, Mrs. Calhoun. She rambled on about a number of friends and their doings and finally ended with a suggestion that it wouldn't hurt if once in a while Jen looked in on her son.

Well, she'd planned on doing just that. Tonight, she'd decided they were going to resolve their differences, one way or the other. Jen's conversation with Ellis, plus time apart had given her a completely different perspective on things. Conversation between them was well overdue putting closure to their unfinished business.

Tre's stereo was cranked way up as usual, meaning he must be home. A few weeks ago she would have been banging on his walls and calling him an inconsiderate SOB. Now she found his music and his presence reassuring.

Jen exited 5C and approached the door of 5B. She rapped sharply.

The volume lowered a bit. She thought she heard

the sounds of approaching footsteps and made sure
to stand in an area directly outside of his vision.

"Who is it?" Tre called.

"Security," she answered, disguising her voice.

"Does security have a name?"

Jen stepped directly in front of the door and Tre's
front door swung open almost immediately.

"I thought you'd left town," he said, his eyes
sweeping over her. "That new hairstyle looks good
on you."

"Thank you. Yes, I was out of town. May I come in?"

He moved aside and in the living room they stared
awkwardly at each other.

"May I sit down?" Jen finally asked.

"Of course."

Tre waved her to a couch. When she sat he joined
her. He was so close she was able to smell the musky
scent of man. She was having difficulty putting her
thoughts in order.

"I heard you might be leaving WARP," Jen began,
forcing the words out. "It's rumored you got a job
with another station."

"That's true but I haven't decided what I want to
do. My moving or not moving will be determined by
a number of different factors."

"Like?"

"Like what WARP comes up with for a package.

Like whether the woman I'm interested in would move with me, and that's just a few of my concerns."

"I see."

He was staring directly at her as if expecting a bigger reaction to his comment about the woman. She decided two could play the same game.

"Which woman would this be? The one that might or might not move with you?"

"My next-door neighbor," Tre said, boldly.

Jen quirked one eyebrow. He was still one cocky son of a gun and sure of himself, too. "And what if this woman likes it here at Flamingo Beach and enjoys her job?"

"A wise man would be respectful of that. He'd even think of commuting for a while. Compromise makes for a good relationship."

"Gee, the last I recall," Jen said, standing and pretending to look baffled, "the woman next door was being accused of some pretty heinous things. Things like deception, wanting to further her own career at the man's expense, buttering up his mother…"

"Ouch!"

Tre was up alongside her and placed his hand over her mouth. "Okay, okay. I admit it. I missed you. Can you blame a brother for being distrustful? I'm a radio personality and I get pursued by some pretty weird types. But time apart gave me a chance to think about how much you've become a part of my life. Of course, you getting along with my mother is a definite plus," he said with a laugh. "But seriously, I really, really missed you."

He removed his palm allowing her to speak.

"I've missed you, too," she said.

Tre kissed her, cutting off any further response she might have made.

"I might be in love," Tre whispered in her ear. "Want to know who with?"

"If you'd like to tell me."

"That sexy woman in 5C. That diva's really gotten under my skin."

"Then maybe you should tell it to *Dear Jenna,* baby. She'd listen."

Tre let loose with a hearty laugh.

"So you think I can entice the woman to stay over?" he asked.

"If you talk to her nicely and whisper the right words in her ear."

"What about if I promise to love her forever and ever."

"That's a good start."

"And what if I told her I missed her and her sexy ways."

"Keep talking, boy!"

Tre was slowly dancing her up the hallway toward the bedroom.

"I think I might be in love, too," Jen confided.

"With who?" Incredulity registered in his voice.

"This fine specimen of a man who lives in 5B. He calls himself D'Dawg. I'm thinking of taking him on this cruise that I won courtesy of his radio station."

"He's onboard. There's a bottle of Red Stripe in his hand. He's on that conga line."

Tre leaned in for another soulful kiss. Jen blocked out the picture of Chere on the dock in her itsy-bitsy bikini screaming, "This ain't fair!"

She'd make it up to her assistant somehow. Right now her priorities lay elscwhere.

She and Tre would do some serious talking in bed about their future. Whatever the outcome she would support him fully. New York was only a two and a half hour flight away and if they planned carefully they could see each other often. It was after all a modern day and commuting couples were common.

They'd reached the bedroom. Tre was already getting undressed.

"Come on, baby," he said, arms wide open.

She took one look at the man she loved. His smooth brown perfectly proportioned body beckoned. If there was one last lingering doubt it fell away.

She loved this man. Heart, body and soul.

FORGED OF STEELE

The sizzling miniseries from
USA TODAY bestselling author

BRENDA JACKSON

*Sebastian Steele's takeover of
Erin Mason's fledgling company
topples when Erin takes over
Sebastian's heart*

NIGHT HEAT

AVAILABLE SEPTEMBER 2006
FROM KIMANI™ ROMANCE

Love's Ultimate Destination

AVAILABLE JANUARY 2007
BEYOND TEMPTATION

Available at your favorite retail outlet.

Leila Owens didn't know
how to love herself let alone
an abandoned baby
but Garret Grayson knew
how to love them both.

She's My Baby

Adrianne Byrd

(Kimani Romance #10)

AVAILABLE SEPTEMBER 2006

FROM KIMANI™ ROMANCE

Love's Ultimate Destination

Available at your favorite retail outlet.

He found *trouble* in paradise.

Mason Sinclair's visit to Barbados was supposed to be about uncovering family mysteries not the mysteries of Lianne Thomas's heart.

EMBRACING
THE MOONLIGHT
(Kimani Romance #12)

Wayne Jordan

AVAILABLE SEPTEMBER 2006
FROM KIMANI™ ROMANCE

Love's Ultimate Destination

Available at your favorite retail outlet.